The Dream Escape

WILLIAM CERVANTES

The Great Escape

By William Cervantes

This is a work of fiction, names, characters, places, and incidents either are the product of the author's imagination or are used fictitiously. Any resemblance to actual persons, living or dead, events, or locales is entirely coincidental.

Copyright © 2021 by William Cervantes

ISBN: 978-0-578-89961-9

Printed in the United States of America

Edited by Zoe Plait

Illustrations by Adrian Arvizu

First Paperback Edition

For my parents, sister, and all of my family.

A special thanks to Adrian Arvizu and Zoe Plait for being an awesome team. They did amazing work and with them this dream became a reality.

TABLE OF CONTENTS

CHAPTER 1: TRAILBLAZER

A man rode his horse on a cool desert night. He was hoping to hit the city of Los Angeles. It was 1922 and many folks were losing hope to be happy. The city of L.A. was only a rumor. A.J. Walker rode his horse until dawn to see the mysterious town.

A.J. was a showman. He would mystify a group with magic performances on the street for spare change. Crowds by the dozens would gather to see his levitating body. He would awe audiences of all ages. A.J. would make an apple disappear and reappear in a madam's bag.

A.J. saved his earnings to buy a small building in Los Feliz. He performed his magic onstage to groups of people. The building doubled as a stage for theatrical guests and plays. However, A.J. was losing mobility in his legs. He wanted to create a reality that fed the imagination. He went on to create the perfect escape room that defied all senses. Right before he was able to showcase his work, he died of a heart attack.

100 years passed. The building was given to the grandson of A.J. The grandson inspected the building before selling it. When he went inside, he was in awe of the beauty his grandpa had created. The grandson, Mr.

Walker, took out some funds and restored the building. When Mr. Walker thought the building was ready, he made a Grand Opening.

It was a beautiful day in L.A. The sun broke through the smog to form a soft orange glow. A warm 94 degrees Fahrenheit outside, it was a perfect day for sandals and shorts. It was summertime and people could feel the good vibrations. The warmth of the sun beamed on a quaint gray building. It was nestled in the city, away from the suburbs.

It was a building so perfect it seemed odd. The neighbor to the right of the building was a beautiful, brick-layered home with windows showing brightly colored drapes. On the other side stood a corporate center with well-tailored businessmen rushing in and out of the office space. They always had a phone up to their ear, promising deals. The corporate center was white and 14 stories high. Complimenting the business center were floor-to-wall windows with a thin aluminum bezel. A beautiful fountain sat directly in the center. It had a water show circled by seating for a pleasing smoke break or conversation with a companion.

Then there was the cube. It was a stubby square building between the other two. A.J. was in love with dice. He was fascinated by chance and luck. Hell, people even wager on chance. A.J. incorporated many straight edges and perfect squares in his designs. To him, dice could be magnified a hundred-fold and still look in perspective. The front entrance was impressive: it had two brown doors, and small windows on each of the sides. White letters were above the door. The sign said, "The Great Escape."

If one were lucky enough to walk through the doors, they would see a dull lobby. In the left corner sat a sad, empty tan couch, possibly leather or suede. Beside the couch was an end table. Placed on the table were a couple of magazines and a leafy green potted plant. The building was gigantic and had more than a lobby. More space had to exist inside the desolate walls. When someone was inside the lobby, they could not see beyond 20 feet. Darkness lurked on the other side. Surprisingly, only one light bar hung from the ceiling, dangling on chains. Two light switches pointed down on the right side of the door.

A young couple held hands while walking and talking to each other on the streets of L.A. The young couple enjoyed a serene Saturday evening stroll. Luckily, they both had the day off and could spend time with each other. The man wore dark blue jeans and a pastel shirt. A graphic on his shirt showed the middle of a street with palm trees lining both sides.

He was confident and direct. When he had a goal in mind, no external force could veer his course. He had All-Stars on his feet and a gait so strong people wondered where his confidence came from. The woman next to him was wearing acid-washed jeans that had scuffs on the knees. The pants were pressed tightly against her skin. She wore TOMs because she liked that they gave to the less fortunate. She was a worldly woman who was selfless and helped other people that had poor circumstances in life. She was wearing a low-cut red blouse that popped brightly.

Together, they approached the corporate center. The man that was with the girl mockingly took out his phone and started to talk into it. He argued that funds had to be transferred into another account and that deadlines had to be met. Someone had to worry about the bottom line. How else would the corporate leaders make their nut?

While passing the fountain, the two felt the ground shake violently. The woman clasped onto the man's arm to avoid falling. A small earthquake had struck! The rumble was strong enough to make them collapse to their knees. This was the strongest earthquake either of them had ever experienced. When the worst had passed, the couple tried to get their senses back. They walked over to the fountain to take a seat. The two switched gears in their conversation.

"Andrea, I don't know what I'd do if the power went out! I'm simple. I ain't no survivor man that could live off the land. My food will spoil in a couple of days with no electricity! I mean, as long as I don't open the fridge door, the food may be cold for awhile."

"Eric, calm down. You're just panicking, but if you really want to survive, fill the bathtub with water." Eric looked at her as a vibrant light bulb went off in his eyes. "And jump in holding a toaster under your arm," she said, smirking at him. His face scrunched up.

Another couple walked towards Andrea and Eric. They looked a little older, but not by much. The other couple had a shaken look in their eyes, and a thousand-yard stare filled their pupils. Eric turned to them and said, "Wow, what a crazy earthquake, huh?" The man stared at Eric quizzically.

His eyebrow raised high, he said, "I didn't feel an earthquake, was it recent?"

Eric was baffled.

"Yeah, like five minutes ago. It was so strong it threw my girlfriend and me to the ground."

"Weird. Maybe a big rig drove on the freeway overpass. They can get loud and scary. I didn't feel anything."

"Oh, uh, well, have a good day," Eric said, stumbling over his words.

The couple relaxed by the fountain until they were ready to start walking. They walked along the sidewalk. They headed in the direction of the grey, cubed building. Their stroll became slower when they approached the peculiar building. It had a *Grand Opening* banner in front. The couple stood near the entrance. *The Great Escape* was displayed above the door. A sign was placed next to the door. *Come explore a law-defying attraction. Stay for the games and puzzles.*

They looked at each other and thought this could be a fun idea. The lure of the unknown enticed them. Eric led the way and started to slowly push the door open. They saw a dim room. Andrea looked at the furniture and walked towards it. She sat on the beige couch. The couch could have been a little more comfortable. She tried adjusting herself to the seat, but she found it uncomfortable.

Eric saw the light switch panel and noticed both switches were flipped down. He leaned in closer and saw tiny words above each switch. The left switch was clearly etched with a hand engraver. It said, "Lights". He glanced over to the right switch and a sticker had the word "Structure." Without thinking, he flipped on the left switch. Immediately, the room was flooded with light and all the walls were visible. There was a teller's window located directly in front of them. The walls were pale blue, nothing vibrant. There was a painting on the wall with a pair of red dice and white dots.

Eric strutted towards the window. In front of Eric was a drawer and a two-way mirror. He saw only his reflection. It gave him a chance to check himself out in the mirror. He looked at his body, clothing, and hair style. A voice boomed from behind. "$13.75 per person.

No refunds. Everyone must sign this waiver. If you decide to accept the challenge, a wavy road lies ahead."

Eric asked, "What is this place?" The teller responded, "Well, if you MUST know,it is a maze, and only the astute can reach the end. It is the perfect escape room."

"Oh, I thought it was a movie theatre."

Eric could hear a chuckle behind the glass. "No, each room has a trick. You have to solve your way out."

The drawer flung open. Eric pulled out his Visa and laid it softly inside the drawer. The drawer slid back into the window, then popped out again with his card, a receipt, and two papers. The papers had lines for signatures.

Eric signed both and handed them back. Andrea had gotten up and walked around while the exchange was happening. She went over to the light switch and turned on the right switch. A jolt went through their bodies as a giant steel door appeared and unlocked itself. They were positive that there were no doors when they first walked in, and they looked at each other in confusion.

"I just finished paying for the maze. What happened?" asked Eric.

"I don't know, I flicked the other light switch and this door appeared next to us. Do you think we should go in?" Andrea asked.

"I heard it unlock, so sure. Let's start the maze."

The couple walked through together as a booming voice came overhead and spoke. "Welcome to The Great Escape. Let your mind grow when you water it, but don't soil it. Too much can be deadly." The intercom announcement ended.

The couple walked into a room. In the room were a table and two chairs on each side. They walked over to sit at the table. When they sat down, each chair quickly darted to the left by itself. The couple hit the floor and slammed their asses against the ground. Thinking it was a coincidence, they tried again, and the chairs moved again! Eric tried to grab the chair to control its position, but the chair scooted away from his grasp. Andrea tried to touch the chair, but it moved slightly out of her reach.

They were like magnets of opposite polarity. The chairs would not allow the couple to make contact. Eric and Andrea decided to give up and look at the objects on the table.

Two keys were displayed next to a carved jade dragon. Eric reached for the key to the left and Andrea walked around the table. There was a small drawer on the bottom of the table. She walked over and started to open the drawer, and a small pair of pliers revealed themselves. When she picked them up, nothing happened.

"Andrea, look at this key when I touch it. It turns into complete mush!"

Her face grew puzzled. Eric was mystified by the key.

"I'm going to pick it up," Eric said. He grabbed the key and set it in the middle of his palm. The bronze key turned into a bronze puddle. "It's not melting. It's cool to the touch," Eric said.

"Well put it back on the table, you fool," Andrea instructed. He started to pour the key back onto the table. What was once a key was now a globule of metal. They both had dumbfounded looks on their faces. The key started to rebuild itself into its original structure. The molecules slowly assembled themselves to the shape of a key. The key's structure had memory. It was returning to its original shape.

The couple took a step back with caution. Andrea stared at the other key, wondering what weird capabilities it had compared to the first. Her curiosity got the best of her and she slowly reached toward the object. She held it in her hand and stared at it closely. It looked like a normal key. It started to change when she brought it up to her face. The key was growing larger in size!

It grew to the size of a coconut before she threw it back on the table. Andrea stared at the cursed object. She poked it a couple of times, but couldn't figure out what had just happened. However, the key did not go back to its original size.

"Geez, what did we get ourselves into?" Eric asked.

"We? I didn't sign up for anything," Andrea retorted.

"I guess I should tell you that I signed for you when he gave me these papers or waivers or whatever..."

"What the fuck, Eric! Did you at least read them?"

"Yes! I read the title. It clearly said waiver."

Andrea was silent. "Yes?"

"I honestly have nothing to say to you."

"Oh c'mon, it's gonna be fun! It's not like we're gonna die."

"Whatever." Andrea reached into her pocket for her phone. She checked the time. It read 1:35 p.m., but when she looked at her service section, it did not have a signal.

"Hey, do you have cell signal in here?" The worry in her voice became more apparent.

"Hmm, lemme check. Nope. No bars."

When Eric finished talking, Andrea's nerves tensed.

"What did that guy tell you? Anything that could help us?" Andrea asked.

"He said only the astute can see the end. I guess we have to look good doing the maze," Eric responded.

"That's not what astute means."

Andrea thought to herself, *Oh god, we are going to die in here.* "This reminds me of *Alice in Wonderland*," she told Eric.

He scoffed. "Please, that's only a movie. None of those things are real." He turned his attention to the jade carving. "That is a pretty neat dragon. It's so intricate. I wonder if it's real stone?"

Eric was puzzled by the dragon. He examined it and decided to pick it up. While holding the dragon, the enlarged key started to shrink! He gasped and put the dragon back on the table. When he put the dragon down, the key stopped shrinking.

Andrea watched Eric the whole time and was also amazed. Eric stepped back from the table and Andrea got closer. She picked up the jade dragon without fear. The key grew smaller again, until it returned to its original size.

"Wow, quite the trick they have set up. There must be a sensor on the dragon. But I can't quite explain the key," Andrea pronounced.

The couple walked around the room to see if any clues existed. The room was of mid-century English design. The walls were eggshell with dark-stained walnut outlining the trim of the walls and ceiling. The lamps were a dark brown glass that covered the bulb, which gave the room a subtle, lively atmosphere. No windows in the entire room existed, which gave it a feeling of being in a basement. Only one other door was in the room. Adjacent on both sides of the door were keyholes. The keyhole to the left was a foot tall. The other was the size of a normal door lock.

"Whoa, do you see how big that keyhole is?" Eric asked Andrea.

"Hmm, that does seem awfully big. Well, I guess we have our first clue. One key must be big enough to fit in that hole. I could probably stick my hand in there," Andrea answered.

"We should probably do a couple tests to see how those two keys react. Those objects are complex and advanced. I haven't seen this technology before. But whatever it is, it's badass. Once we get out, I am gonna look up who built this place, for sure," Eric stated.

Andrea and Eric walked back to the table where it all started.

"I'm sure that door is our way out. The door we came in through is gone," Andrea told Eric.

"Huh, would you look at that. It is gone." Eric walked back to where they entered and felt the wall with his hand. He started tapping the wall to hear if any hollow noises existed, but it was completely solid. "The door is gone. There's no trace of it anywhere." Eric walked back to the only other door in the room. He noticed something written at the bottom of the door. It said, "One option makes you larger, and one option makes you smaller."

"Hey Andrea, come check this out!"

She walked over to Eric and read what he pointed at. "That's pretty interesting. I know those keys must go into those locks. It makes sense, right? Like one key got bigger and the other melted. We just have to find out the best way to do it."

The couple had a common goal to accomplish. Their heads acted as one unit.

"Let's go for the big one first," Eric told Andrea. "I will grab the key because who knows if it gets heavier. It shouldn't, but who knows in this place? And of course, I have way bigger muscles than you do," Eric said with a condescending smirk.

"Let me grab the dragon and see if it shrinks any smaller," Andrea said. She walked over and picked up the dragon. They both looked at the key, but the key shrank just a tiny bit smaller to its original size. Eric shrugged and walked over to the key to pick it up. The key stayed the same size while he held it. The couple stared at each other.

"Well, that was different. Here, let me put the dragon down." Andrea set the dragon down.

Eric started to feel a warmth coming from his hand as the key started to mutate. Exactly like before, the key started growing. It grew larger and larger, first to the size of a tennis ball, then a melon, then to the size of a basketball. It became too heavy for Eric. His arms hung close to the ground before he let go and the key made a thud on the floor.

"What the hell! The key started getting heavier. That's impossible! I don't know what nutjob created this place, but it sure doesn't behave like anything I've ever seen before," Eric stated.

Andrea replied, "This place is weird. First the chairs, and now the keys. I don't think we should expect anything different going forward." Eric nodded in agreement.

Andrea picked up the small dragon. Once she held the dragon, the key started to shrink on the floor. She held it until it was the size of a tennis ball. Eric approached the key. He picked it up and tossed it quickly back on the table like a hot potato wrapped in tin foil. When the key landed, it remained the same exact size.

"It looks like I have to hold it for it to get bigger. But we also know it doesn't grow when you hold the dragon at the same time. It does not help us with the other key," Eric said.

Andrea was curious and walked over to the other key. She poked it with her finger, and nothing happened. She poked it again; still nothing. Andrea decided to leave her finger a little longer on the key. A puddle slowly formed around her finger. Little ripples originated from her finger and spread throughout the key. When she removed her finger from the key, the ripples slowed down. It turned back into a solid.

The key morphed back into its original shape. Eric walked over and picked up the key. He held it in his palm while he looked at it intently. The key started to melt in his hands. It lost its outline of sharp teeth. The pins had to perfectly align with the teeth on the key for the lock to open.

The couple needed the perfect configuration to unlock both mechanisms. The enlarged lock could not be too big or too small for the locking feature to open. The other challenge was to keep the other key from melting.

Eric noticed the outline of the teeth disappearing into a pool of metal. After ten seconds of holding the key, the metal melted into a liquid. He moved his hand and saw the metal swirling in circles. He waved Andrea over to look at the characteristics of the newly-formed metal.

She poked the metal in his hand and her finger sank in. The material did not stick to her skin; it slid right off.

"Wow, that sure is weird. It's completely liquid! I saw the same thing when I held my finger on it. But it didn't all melt. The place where my finger was started to get softer," Andrea told Eric.

"Yeah, this stuff is weird. It reminds me of mercury. It's completely liquid at room temperature, but when you add heat, its properties change," Eric responded.

He plopped it on the table. The key squished and flattened on the table. It splashed like water hitting concrete. The key spread to the size of a dinner plate. The edges of the metal pool hardened. It took a while for the key to restore to its original shape. Finally, after morphing, it looked perfect. The key had no indications it had melted.

"I have no idea how we're going to prevent it from melting like that. Maybe if we melt it in a pot? It may look like a soup at first, but can we pour it into the keyhole? It could grow to the pins of the lock." Eric said.

"Yeah, that doesn't sound like a bad idea. We just have to find a pot first. We could look around."

The couple searched the room. They walked along the edges and the middle of the room. In the room was only a door, a table, and the chairs. There were no couches, seats, or even end tables. Andrea walked closer to the table and remembered the drawers in the table. She got closer and opened the drawer. The first drawer she opened was empty. She closed it and opened the other.

There were the pliers. The pot idea inspired Andrea. She thought if they did not touch the key, it would not melt.

"Eric! Come look at this." Eric walked over to Andrea as she grabbed the pliers.

The pliers stayed open until she squeezed the handles. They closed to a tight fit. Andrea closed and opened them a couple times to get a feel of how they closed. Immediately, she walked towards the melting key on the table.

She barely touched the key with the pliers. No reaction. She held the pliers on the key for a couple more seconds. The key did not melt; it stayed perfectly solid.

"Hah! Take a look! The key isn't melting anymore. The tips of the pliers are touching the edge of it and it isn't changing shape. Let me put them in the middle." Andrea tried to drive the pliers through the key. The pliers did not penetrate the key. The key pushed back on the pliers and there was no change in its shape.

"I think I know what we're supposed to do," Andrea told Eric. She pushed the key to the edge of the table. The handle of the key hung off the table. She opened the pliers and closed the tips to grab the end of the key. She grabbed the key with the tool and held it up in the air. The key did not change shape. It looked like a perfectly normal key. But in the building A.J. Walker created, nothing was absolute, and science got turned upside down. Physics were twisted and turned and thrown into a taffy machine. Everything they knew about Earth and its environment was now wrong. Their minds were perceiving reality in a new dimension.

Andrea held the key with the pliers and walked carefully to the lock. She tried her hardest not to drop the key. She aimed the key towards the lock. With a little bit of force, the key entered the lock. Andrea felt the lock get loose with a click, and she was able to turn it sideways. She let go and raised her hands in the air. "Yes! Look, it fit perfectly in this one!"

"Awesome!" Eric shouted back.

She walked over to him. "We just have to figure out how we can get that second lock," Andrea said.

"We're gonna have to work together. I have an idea. I will hold the key while you hold the dragon. Hopefully, the key will stay the same size while I get it closer to the lock. When I put the key in, drop the dragon on the table and wait until I signal for you to pick it back up. We will try to match the size of the key and the lock," Eric said.

Andrea agreed with the plan. The couple walked over to their respective objects. Andrea grabbed the dragon and held it above the table. Eric grabbed the key; it did not grow. He was pleased, and he smiled. He walked towards the door. He held the key somewhere in the middle of the opening on the bigger lock.

"When I say NOW, drop the dragon on the table," Eric commanded.

"Okay, sounds good," Andrea replied.

"Okay, I have the key in place. Now!"

Andrea dropped the dragon on the table. She did not anticipate the statue to bounce away from her. It rolled to the other end of the table. Andrea quickly realized the dragon was farther than her arms could reach, and she ran after the dragon.

The key grew larger. He had waited until it was the right size. Eric pushed the key into the lock, but the key had grown too large! The key bounced back. It kept growing larger. Eric was losing his grip. He could not hold the key any longer and dropped it on the floor. The wood underneath him cracked from the impact.

"Holy shit, that would've broken my foot," Eric said cautiously. Eric thought for a second. The timing needed to be perfect, unless he let the key grow into the lock. He thought it might be possible for the key to break the lock if it got too big.

Andrea finally picked the dragon back up and the key started to shrink. He looked back at her. "What happened?" Eric asked.

"Sorry, that was totally my fault. I dropped it too high, and it bounced away from me. I'll make sure to drop it closer." She smiled at him.

"Let's try again. The key got too big and would not go into the lock. I want to try to leave it in until the key grows into the lock. But you're gonna have to be fast. I don't want the lock to break and leave us trapped in here." Andrea gave him a thumbs up.

Eric picked up the key and put it back in the middle. "Okay, drop the dragon." When the dragon hit the table, the key started to grow. It began to fill the shape of the lock. Eric yelled out, "Soon!" He felt the edges of the key touch the lock. "Now!" Andrea placed the dragon on the table. Eric let go of the key and stepped back. He looked closely and gave the key a turn. It started to turn. The key was able to rotate all the way. The couple was ecstatic.

Eric was bold. He led with his gut and let his head follow. His actions were confident - sometimes too confident. Growing up, he was a very creative boy, but he was not fond of school. Eric did not like the idea of taking tests. He thought they were a poor metric to judge someone's aptitude of learning. Eric constantly talked back to teachers and acted like a smartass.

Sports did not grab his attention, but he did hang out with the popular crowds. He hung out with his friends from the cul-de-sac and stuck with them. Things changed when they all graduated high school, and the friends lost touch with one another.

Eric was an artist. He enjoyed exploring the creative depths of his mind. He attended community college, but did not make strides. He only took the classes that he thought were interesting, not ones that put him on a degree path. But Eric was not a fool. His curiosity pushed him to learn all kinds of topics. If he applied himself, he could reach heights higher than other people could ever achieve. Unfortunately, a dash of laziness and a sprinkle of short attention span held him back.

Andrea was quite the opposite growing up. She was a bit of a loner. Her lunches were spent with a book, away from the other children. She was studious and outperformed all her classmates. After her sophomore year of high school, she cared more about the way she looked than the grades she got. The classes were never too hard for her. Boys started to notice her more and went up to her to start conversations. The new attention was a change for her.

She had no serious boyfriend in high school. She eventually made close friends with other girls towards her senior year. They kept in touch and got brunch every now and then. Andrea appreciated them a lot and felt they helped her through tough times. Her major was communications and she attended UCLA. After lots of thought, she wanted to become a journalist. The status quo had to be changed, and she wanted a perspective that would shock readers. Andrea was an outstanding person. She wanted to give the real story of what was happening out in the world. She hated the clickbait culture that was running amuck on smart devices.

Andrea viewed people in two different categories: The dimmers and the shiners, just like an old Vegas sign lit up by hundreds of lightbulbs. Each light bulb was a person. Some were very dim and did not produce much light. Hell, some bulbs were not even on. But the shiners made the sign pop, and without them there would be no pizazz.

Andrea and Eric looked at each other and were curious to know what the other door held behind it. Andrea told Eric, "I guess we should keep going? I don't know if this is going to end anytime soon." Eric agreed and pushed open the door.

CHAPTER 2: FAULTY SENSORS

The couple walked through the door and into a new room. They stared at a bed that was located in the center of the room. It had a pink fluffy blanket that laid across the king-sized bed. The headboard was a precious piece of oak with hand carvings of vines. There were beautiful hand-carved oak posts on either side.

Carved in the center was the body of a voluptuous woman. The headboard resembled a large grape vine. It was inlaid with a neat gold trim that highlighted the edges of every intricate wood piece. Sturdy, comfortable, and bespoke, it was a luxury only wealthy people knew. Comfort and peace of mind could exist in the bed. The headboard had words painted on it.

"The king sleeps while he sends his armies to fight his battles," Eric read out loud.

Eric got closer to the bed and ran his fingers across the blanket. He tried to pick it up.

"Holy hell, this is heavy. I wanted to nap. It feels like one of those weighted blankets you always wanted. You know, it's not even that comfy. It feels like it's stuffed with hay," Eric said.

Andrea let Eric fool around with the bed. Andrea walked closer to the headboard.

"Whoa, the detail on this headboard is amazing. It must've taken someone a very long time to make this."

I wonder what the gimmick is here, Andrea thought. Eric tried removing the pink blanket, but he couldn't carry it by himself. There was nothing else in the room except the bed and another door. They couldn't go backwards. The couple knew they had to keep moving forward. Eric sat on the bed and started swinging his legs.

"So whatcha think? Maybe we are supposed to nap? Or, you know..." He gave Andrea seductive eyes.

Andrea blushed. "No, Eric, not in public. And who knows · they probably have cameras in here." Eric shrugged and thought he could at least try.

"Well, do you have any bright ideas?" Eric asked. Andrea began to ponder while walking closer to the bed.

"Wow, this isn't comfortable at all." She could barely lift the blanket an inch off the bed without straining.

"Geez, what's this made of? Concrete?" Andrea looked a little closer at the bed. The bed was sunken in the middle. It looked like a chunk of the bed was missing. She climbed on the bed and poked the center. The pink blanket caved in. Andrea jumped off the bed and put her hand underneath her chin.

"Hey meathead, come here," Andrea said, smiling at Eric. He stood next to her. "I know we can't lift the blanket - it's way too heavy, even though it shouldn't be. But what if we just slide it off?" Eric looked at Andrea and nodded in agreement. They both stood at the end and grabbed a corner with both hands.

"Okay, on three," Andrea said. "One, two, three..."

Andrea pulled with all of her strength and the blanket didn't budge. "Ahhh!" Andrea yelled, and shot piercing eyes at Eric. He grinned and said sorry.

"I thought you meant *after* three."

Andrea shook her head in disappointment. "Okay, one more time. One, two, three, pull!" They both dug their heels into the floor and used all the muscles in their arms. The blanket only moved a couple of inches. They stopped to take a breather. They noticed a shining blue light coming from the center of the bed. They knew they were on the right path. The couple had gotten in sync and pulled the blanket rhythmically, like rowers trying to get to the finish line. The blanket was halfway off, and the blue light beamed from the center.

The couple gave one last tug and pulled the blanket right off the bed. The blanket fell from its own weight and hit the floor. They investigated the center of the bed where the light was shining. They noticed a bunch of empty circles recessed into the bed. Eric was confused, but he touched one of the circles.

A blue plastic token appeared out of thin air and landed in the spot he touched. The couple laughed, and another plastic token appeared and landed in another spot. The other token was red. The couple was amused as they watched the tokens land. Eric took a step back and looked at the circles from a distance.

"Ha! It's a Connect Four board. That's great! See, I told you this would be fun. It's just a friendly game. I wonder if they have Jenga in this joint. I would totally kick your ass."

"Yeah, right. When you start losing you knock over the tower before you can accept your defeat." Eric snarled at Andrea after her comment.

"Should we play together or take turns against the computer?"

"I think you should go, mister all-high-and-mighty. Let's see your chops."

Eric smiled and continued to touch the next available spot. Two tokens fell and it was Eric's turn again. He tried to use strategy, and selected another spot. Two more coins fell. "Aww, c'mon, he totally blocked me. Don't worry, I'll get him soon. I got a couple of tricks up my sleeve." The game continued and turns went by.

Right before Eric was going to make his turn, he heard, "You idiot, you lost!" Eric stopped and looked at the board. The opponent had beaten him. Eric put his head down and selected his losing spot. The last red token fell, and the computer won the game. The middle of the square turned bright red and flashed a couple of times. The plastic tokens fell to the bottom. When the tokens hit the floor, the room started shaking violently.

"Earthquake?" Andrea asked.

The walls moved a foot closer to the bed, making the room a lot smaller.

"Well, that's not a good sign."

"You idiot, you're gonna get us killed!"

"Ah, whatever. They wouldn't do that. They are just trying to get us scared."

"Fine. It's my turn anyways."

Andrea leaned over the bed and touched one of the empty circles. A red and blue token appeared and landed in two different spots. The game continued and Eric watched. Andrea noticed she was being beaten but did not say anything. Right until the last turn, Andrea was quiet.

"Shit, I think I lost."

"Where?" Eric asked. Andrea pointed at the empty slots showing where the machine beat her. She made her last turn and the bed flashed red. The walls closed in closer to the couple.

"Okay, we've really got to beat this guy. The walls are pretty close to us."

"Why don't we play together? Two heads are better than one." They both decided on the first spot. Two tokens fell from the sky. They played a couple turns and realized the difficulty was much harder than anticipated. Turns and turns passed by. At the end, they lost the game, and the walls closed in. The walls were only an arm's distance away from the couple.

"This is a lot harder than I thought. This thing keeps beating us. But I don't think we have a choice, since there's no door in here. Okay, one last time." Andrea said.

The couple hunkered down and meticulously thought of every move against their assailant. They slowly decided every move as if they were war generals strategically placing troops against enemy lines. At the end of the game, they saw the opening. They were able to connect four! The couple pointed to the winning spot and the token fell in. Lights flashed blue in their favor. They were thrilled and hugged each other deeply while the walls started to retreat to their original position. While the walls moved back, a door appeared behind a wall. They knew they must continue. The entrance was long gone and there was no way of going back now.

They turned the doorknob. The door slowly creaked open and a bright light emitted from the edges of the door. Brightness enveloped their vision while their eyes tried to adjust. They were astounded: the door opened outside to a wide-open field of roses. Only ten feet in front of them was a thorny wall of beautifully colored roses.

A labyrinth awaited inside the wall of roses. They scoured the wall to find an entrance. Walking in a frenzy, their pace suddenly slowed down. Eric grabbed Andrea's hand and led the way. His confidence made up for his idiocy. Andrea clamped tight; she did not want to let him go.

"Hey, can you stop for a bit? I want to smell the flowers!" Andrea exclaimed.

"Sure thing," Eric answered. Andrea approached the center of a flower with her nose. She pulled away quickly, scrunched up her face, and looked extremely displeased.

"What happened? You look constipated," Eric said jokingly.

"It's wretched! Go on, take a whiff."

Eric shrugged his shoulders and leaned in with his nose. "Hot damn! They smell like rotten eggs! For being so pretty, they are revolting."

Eric wanted to touch the flower. He moved his hand closer and touched the petal of the rose. His hand accidentally grazed the thorn. Something was off. The thorn was very soft. He pushed harder and the thorn felt like a plushie. He shook his head and started touching all the thorns harder.

Andrea was confused and did not want to copy his actions. Eric looked back at Andrea, lifted his right eyebrow, and stuck his whole hand into the wall of roses. Andrea was shocked. But she did not hear any cries for help. Eric noticed they all felt soft and cushiony. He started to wave his arm inside the bush. Swinging it in circles, he gasped and left out a chuckle.

"Wow, it's like a pillow! Come check it out. The roses are clouds here."

"I don't know about this. Something does not feel right. Thorns are supposed to hurt, and flowers are supposed to smell good."

"Well, you don't know what you're missing. It feels like a warm blanket."

Andrea worriedly replied, "But what if some of the roses feel like that and the other ones have horns that can hurt you?"

Eric looked at Andrea but dismissed what she said. He turned his back towards the wall of roses and took a couple of steps. He took a running start and dove into the bushes like he was diving into a ball pit. A couple of rose stalks fell over. The jump was over-anticipated, and Eric fell to the ground with roses all around him. Andrea was not pleased and gave him the evil eye. Eric stood back up and brushed the foliage off his shirt.

"You should try it!" Eric yelled.

"No," Andrea said sternly, and put an end to the conversation.

"I wonder what it could mean. Putrid roses and soft thorns..." Andrea mused.

"Why does everything have to have a meaning? Why can't it just be?" Eric questioned.

"Reality doesn't work that way," Andrea said.

"Stop being so logical. Picasso's paintings don't look like real people for a reason."

Andrea's curiosity caused a mental itch. Examining the plants a little closer, she decided to touch a thorn. Her eyes flung open; they were soft. Slowly looking at the flower, she heard a loud rustling from Eric's direction.

Eric was using his hand as a machete. He knocked down the roses in his way, making his own trail. Andrea followed right behind Eric, since she didn't want to risk getting hurt. He chopped down every single rose with no one to stop him. With no sense of direction, he kept going. Time slipped away. The daytime sky started to get darker. The hours seemed to go faster, and the couple had no clear destination ahead.

The sun had disappeared and the night sky loomed down on them. The stars were bright. Eric noticed something odd. There was no familiar constellation.

"We've been here for hours and we haven't moved anywhere, Eric. We're going in circles. Admit it. We're lost." Andrea stopped following Eric. "ERIC!" Andrea snapped at him. He paused and looked with low eyes.

This time Eric was confused. He looked up at the stars. His neck locked into that position. "Huh." Eric thought deeply..

"What is it?"

"Well, I'm looking up, but the stars are all in wrong places. Like, look there." He grabbed Andrea's shoulder and pulled her close to his side. He pointed to the sky."The big dipper should be somewhere along this path." He swept his finger from one horizon to the other. "None of these stars makes sense. It's like they're random." While showing her the stars, his head was next to hers. They stopped looking at the sky and looked at each other. They locked eyes. Eric looked at Andrea's eyes and saw fear. He looked at her eyes and her mouth.

Her lips looked soft, large, and shiny with lip gloss. He licked his lips and she smiled. With the other hand he grabbed her chin and lifted her head up towards him. He leaned in and their lips touched, gently puckering. A small smooch sound came when they pulled away. He squeezed her closer to his side. Eric checked his watch: 3:45pm. His mouth dropped.

"Hey, how long do you think we've been in this garden?" Eric asked.

"I dunno, probably like six hours."

"It's been thirty-five minutes."

They were stunned. "I'm heading back, This is stupid," Andrea grumbled.

"It's a good thing I've been knocking over these bushes so we can see where we started from," Eric said.

They both turned around and looked for the original path. It was gone. The roses stood back up and grew. There was no clear path from where they started. They both felt defeated; the room had won.

Eric sat down on a bed of roses while he played with the dirt next to him. He swirled his finger in it. After one last swirl, he laid down. The thorns felt like a quilt sewn by angels and washed in a river of lavender.

"Come lay down with me. We might as well enjoy how good it feels. And these roses smell amazing. Like fresh new sheets out of the dryer."

Andrea started to get anxious. Her world was closing in on her. Her head started to spin, and the roses felt like they were getting closer and closer to her. Feeling claustrophobic, she sat next to Eric and tried to relax. Her breathing got very fast, and Eric saw her chest rising and sinking quickly. He put one hand on her back and started to rub it.

"Take deep breaths. Pull the oxygen out of the air and let it out with one giant sigh." She followed Eric's instructions and her breathing started to slow down.

"Wait, did you say those roses smell like fresh sheets?"

"Yeah, sniff it," Eric told her.

Dumbfounded, Andrea realized Eric was right. An intuition drove her to smell more roses. She smelled the roses behind Eric. They smelled like fresh picked flowers. Andrea smelled the roses in front of Eric. The foul smell coated the inside of her nose and forced her to gag. Eric giggled.

Andrea looked at him with piercing eyes and his smile quickly vanished from his face. The flowers that smelled amazing drew her attention. The good-smelling ones stuck to a path. Eric stood up and started to follow her.

Smell, hit, smell, hit. Andrea got into a groove while Eric followed blindly. She followed the good-smelling flowers and rejected the odd-smelling ones. The pleasant-smelling flowers led in the correct direction.

"A path!" Andrea yelled in joy.

The couple jumped onto the path. There were a few turns in the route. The couple walked side by side and tried to figure out where it led. Finally, they found an opening.

The roses were all behind them. In front of them was a massive lake. It was the size of a tennis court. The water rippled with very little wind. The waters were rough in this body of water. The dirt that touched the water was moist. This water had a pulsating energy. It was alive. Alive and not calm.

Behind the lake were giant walls that looked like the entrance to the building. Both walked around the lake but kept a keen eye on it. It felt like someone or something was watching them. The couple turned around, but nothing was there. A powerful gaze seemed to record their every move. The feeling was unnerving. They felt a presence along their backs, like someone was about to whisper a secret. A ringing sound hummed in their ears. The ringing lasted for five seconds and then went away.

They walked near the lake and came up to a massive wall. Eric went up and touched it with his hand. He grazed his fingertips along the stucco and gave it a couple of whacks.

"Well, it's definitely solid. I don't see an entrance, though. I wonder if it would lead us back inside?" Eric asked Andrea.

"I wonder if there's anyone in here with us. Like other people who decided to do this weird maze. HELLO!" Eric yelled out to the area and waited for a response.

"I get what you mean. Ever since we saw this lake, it feels like someone else is here, too," Andrea responded.

"Huh, I was feeling the same thing, babe. Maybe they're just shy."

In front of the walls were giant flood lamps that cast light on the whole area. No corner was dark. It was so bright that it simulated daylight. Eric kept walking around the wall. Andrea wandered over to the lake. Eric put his hand against the wall and walked back and forth. He tried to feel different textures on the wall. Eric thought that there could be a hidden door or a hidden handle. But that would be too easy.

He inspected the wall, bringing his face as close as possible. Only the stucco could be seen. Eric took a step back and visualized the wall. He stood in front and started to wave his arms like a mad man. He flapped like a bird ready to take flight.

His shadow mimicked his movements and he chuckled to himself. Eric pulled up his left foot to the inner part of his knee. He brought his hands together with his palms touching and his fingers pointing to the sky. His shadow followed perfectly.

"OOhhhhhhhmmmmm." He decided to chant and focus all his energy to keep his balance. Andrea turned towards Eric and shook her head side to side. She let out a big sigh. "I'm partnered with a child," she murmured under her breath.

"Andrea, check it out! Perfect shadows!" Eric yelled towards her. She looked at him, forced a smile, and gave a thumbs up.

The lake fascinated her; it was a calm environment, but the waves crashed on the shoreline violently. "Where is it getting the power?" she asked herself. Andrea kept walking in circles around the lake. Something caught her eye. The waves crashed and broke in her direction like they were trying to get her wet, or worse, pull her in. The water tracked her around the lake. The lake made Andrea fearful. It seemed to have a mind of its own. A boulder lay next to the lake.

The dragon from the first room sparked a memory in her, and she decided to look under the rock. The words inscribed read, "The darkness will lead to confusion, while the light will lead to glory. On both paths, a struggle shall be fought."

The clue made her head hurt. "It barely makes sense. Like the battle between good and evil? Hmm, I wonder. But why would both paths lead to fighting?" she said to herself. Eric could not hear her. He was very far away and having too much fun with his own shadow.

Eric was having a blast. Being in a new world didn't faze him. He stood up straight and threw up the peace sign. However, this time was different. The shadow remained still and did not reciprocate his peace sign. Eric froze.

A perfect silhouette stood up straight and tall. Eric waved his hand. The shadow waved back. He started to back away slowly, and his shadow on the wall started to get smaller.

"Hey Andrea, are you okay?" he asked.

"Yes. Why, what's up?" Andrea replied.

"Uh, nothing. Just wanted to make sure."

Andrea shrugged and walked closer to Eric. "This water is weird. I feel like it's following me."

"Ha, nonsense. You're probably just imagining things. Sometimes your eyes can play tricks on you." He did not mention the shadow.

"Well, you should at least read this rock." She pointed to the rock and flipped it over. Eric walked to it and read the inscription.

"Hmm, strange. Why would there be a struggle if you are going towards glory?

"It does take a lot of energy to be great," she replied.

"If you were really that great, I think it would come naturally."

"I don't know about that, Eric. Have you ever fully applied yourself?"

"Sure, a bunch of times. That's why I'm so popular," he said with a smile.

"Greatness isn't some popularity contest."

"Then why does it take a lot of people to remember legends? If not, everyone would forget about them."

Andrea stood silent. In Eric's convoluted mind, the argument made sense. He grabbed her hand and pulled her closer to the wall. "Come on, make a shadow puppet. Loosen up a little."

They both walked over to the wall. They got closer and the shadows started to present themselves. They grew bigger and matched the size of the couple. She gave in and made the only shadow puppet she knew. It was a little barking dog. "Woof woof," Andrea said. She moved her fingers to make the cute shadow dog bark. Eric laughed and did little bunny ears. His shadow bunny got closer to the dog. She barked again and the bunny backed away from the dog, frightened.

They giggled together. Andrea went up to the wall and made a small OK sign with her fingers. The shadow followed her movements and made an OK sign as well.

When she puts her hands down, the shadow didn't. The shadow had made a fist!

Andrea stepped back. "Whoa, did you see that?"

"What exactly?" Eric replied.

"I don't know."

They both took a step back and looked at the shadows. Eric raised his hands above his head, but the shadow stood still. It did not follow Eric's movements. The couple froze.

Their shadows started to move. Both shadows started wiggling their arms like they had woken from a great slumber. Both shadows looked at each other. The profile of the heads started to change. Their noses were pronounced. Immediately, Eric and Andrea looked at each other, mimicking the shadows.

The shadows stopped looking at each other and proceeded to turn their heads towards the couple. Eric and Andrea looked back at the shadows. The couple knew they were being stared at. No eyes, no mouth, no nose: just a pure black body. But deep down, all four entities knew they were staring at each other. The couple took a step back, but the shadows remained the same size. The shadows looked at each other once again and nodded. They reached for their own dark legs and grasped them tightly. The shadows pulled their legs off the wall and broke free from the wall. The shadows were in the couple's realm.

The shadows didn't have masters or puppeteers; they had minds of their own. Andrea stood closer to Eric. He wrapped his arm around her and pulled her waist in closer.

"Easy. They're using a projector," Eric said. Eric's shadow walked closer to Eric. Its left foot stepped away from the wall and stepped on the ground. The shadows rose to become three-dimensional creatures. The shadow broke the constraints of living on the wall.The two creatures of pure darkness stood in front of the couple.

Bold, dark, and ominous, they were people with no features. They had mass because the grass beneath the shadow people crunched and changed shape. They were capable of action. Andrea's jaw dropped to the ground. The shadows walked closer. The couple bolted in the other direction, back into the maze of roses.

"WHAT THE FUCK WAS THAT?" Andrea yelled with fear.

"Shh, they're gonna hear you."

"Are you kidding me? They're shadows. They don't have ears."

"Hey, I don't know what they're capable of. For all I know, they can shoot lasers out of their eyes. Those fucking things just turned to life."

"For fuck's sake, this is scary. We're not even inside anymore. Who knows how far this place stretches?"

"Wait, be quiet."

The couple stood quietly. They heard rustling leaves. It must have been the shadows, not too far away from them.

"So, what should we do?" whispered Andrea.

"I don't know. For now, just relax. Maybe they will leave," Eric said.

The couple went completely quiet for a couple of minutes. Eventually, the rustling went away. The couple was not too far away from the lake. They could hear the crashing waves. A low voice was flowing through the wind. It sounded like scratches, but the couple could not make out the noise.

"Did you hear that?" Eric asked.

"No." Andrea responded.

"Listen closer." Eric said in a hush voice.

It got louder and turned into a low mumble. Something was trying to communicate with them. All of sudden the noise stopped. The couple looked at each other. They turned their heads to look around. A chill breeze blew on their necks. A shiver tingled their spines. A heavy presence was among them. It felt like a thousand eyes were peering in their direction. A twig snapped behind them and they turned around. The shadows were standing over them like titans. The couple stood up and screamed at the top of their lungs. Their fight-or-flight reflexes allowed them to run and escape. Not looking back, they ran next to each other, pushing through and knocking over any roses in their path. They tried to escape from the peril of the shadows.

They eventually made it back to the lake. The couple slowed down to a stop and bent over to catch their breath. Next to the lake was a perfect white rabbit nibbling on the grass. The bunny looked at the couple with pure red eyes. It was an albino rabbit. The couple was confused. But not too long after, the shadows broke through the wall of roses. The shadows pushed down all the stems to get closer to the couple. The bunny heard the rose stems breaking and looked over at that area. The bunny noticed the shadows and its ears went up. It scattered and went into the lake, disappearing in a flash.

The couple was scared for their lives. "Should we follow that bunny?" Eric asked.

"Only if I'm away from those monsters. I would prefer drowning."

The couple held hands and darted towards the lake where the bunny had vanished. They heard the shadows running right behind them. The shadows were closing in on the couple, and the shadows were faster. Right before the couple ran into the lake, a shadow reached out and grabbed Andrea's hair. Her head jerked back, and she let out a shriek. She turned back and swatted the arm of the shadow. Andrea contacted its arm and it pulled away. As they ran into the lake, Eric raised his left middle finger.

They ran into the middle of the lake without getting wet. A damp darkness swallowed them. It was pitch black and their pace slowed down. They couldn't see two feet in front of them. They took a couple steps forward, but the ground was slippery. The couple fell on their butts and slid down.

"Whoa! I wonder where this is taking us!" Eric yelled.

"I don't know. It feels like the shadows' home," Andrea said worryingly. They slid down with no end in sight.

"I wonder how long this will go for?" Eric asked.

"Yeah, it's taking a while. It's kinda like one of those carnival rides you ride down with the sack underneath."

Eric chuckled. "This is way better than one of those rides. It's lasting forever. At least we got our money's worth."

Andrea stayed quiet, but Eric could feel her eyes rolling to the back of her head. The incline gradually came to an end, and they could feel themselves slowing down. A warm, glowing light could be seen beneath their feet. Eric and Andreas's hopes were restored. They slowed to a halt. Their buttocks finally hit the floor and they reached their destination. They rose to their feet and looked around. It was a normal room, or what seemed normal to them.

There was a door on the other side. Eric looked up and noticed above them was a floating body of water.

"That makes no sense. Look up." Andrea looked up and saw the lake about eight feet above them. In the corner were the two shadows looking at them. The shadows were motionless. Andrea said, "Okay, c'mon. Those things are giving me the fucking creeps." They walked to the door and went into the next room.

CHAPTER 3: LOOSE CONNECTIONS

The couple was surrounded by mantels of deer and moose heads. The rows of antlers lined the wall, all the way to the ceiling. The room looked like a hunter's house that overglorified his achievements. But something was different about these stuffed heads. There was something wrong with their eyes. The couple approached the mantels a little closer. They noticed googly eyes on all the animals. They giggled to each other. The couple walked around the room, soaking the details in. Eric grabbed Andrea's hand. He was extremely comfortable with her and felt at peace when she was close. Andrea looked over and smiled. She felt safe next to Eric. The two had shared many adventures together. They had met over two years previously.

Eric had been in a bookstore looking for content that his brain could munch on. He did not read quickly or well, but he wanted to add more books to his bookcases. His thought was that a bigger library would impress people. Eric was too proud to admit that he had not read over half of them.

He walked down the aisles, looking at different genres. He noticed a girl, cute as could be, sitting on a couch. She immediately caught his eye. Her face was well-defined with a dark complexion. Long, straight, silky, jet-black hair laid perfectly on her shoulders. She was wearing a tight, black, long-sleeved shirt, ripped acid-washed jeans, and a pair of white flats. There she was, drop dead gorgeous. Eric froze for half a second. He wanted to get a good glance at her before she disappeared behind a bookshelf. Eric cherished those milliseconds and squeezed all of them into his memory, like he was squeezing an orange dry to get a sip of juice in the desert sun. The bookshelf covered her from his vision, and he kept on walking.

He paused in between two bookshelves. His brain was in a trance. Feelings of anxiety ran from his fingers to his feet. *What would I say?* Eric thought, trying to run different scenarios in his head. *Do I say hello? What day is it? I guess the weather is fine today, but that's too cliché. Like, it is a good day.* He clenched a book in his hand and tried to figure out what to do. *I could smile, but that's kind of creepy. Maybe like a chuckle to let her know I'm funny? No no no. Wait, I should ask for her name. I want to know her. I need to know her.*

He mustered enough courage to walk in the direction of the girl. The couch where the girl was sitting was vacant. Eric felt destroyed on the inside. *I did all this planning in my head, for what! What a waste of time. I knew it was stupid of me to even attempt such a move.* A big sigh came out and he kept walking towards the next bookshelf. He was in the fiction section, thinking of all the worlds that could be, all of them laid in the pages of the books.

Eric was stuck in a mundane reality that heavily repeated itself. The day-in-and-day-out work life tired him out. Being a car washer did not help. While staring at the titles of the books, he was distracted by a daydream. In Eric's mind, he always won. The thought of going on a coffee date with the mystery woman popped up. The thought of it made him grin. Someone walked at the end of the aisle.

The person walked by too quickly for Eric to see. Before he could turn his head, the person had passed. He shrugged his shoulders, picked up a book, and opened it. The words barely stuck in his head, though he tried to grasp what he read. But he was far too invested in his daydream to even care.

Andrea walked at the end of the aisle, perusing all the books. She loved the history and the idea of writing. The books had the thoughts of great scholars from eras before her time. She loved the smell of old paper and bindings slowly deteriorating. All the books were waiting to spill stories or knowledge to the seeker.

I cannot find anything, Andrea thought to herself. *I want to expand my mind. I should get a nonfiction book. Freud seems popular among people. Maybe I can find out why I am the way I am.* A thought of her parents appeared in her head. She was occupied with her thoughts as she walked by an aisle with a boy looking at the books.

Where is the nonfiction section? Andrea thought, and kept walking.

Each aisle said the name of the genre from a hanging piece of wood. She caught a glimpse of the nonfiction section and started walking in that direction.

There was a smile on her face when she arrived at the nonfiction section. Andrea looked up and down the shelves to see if a book was interesting enough for her mind. She paused in the middle of the aisle to look at the titles with more attention.

Eric walked aimlessly in the store. He did not like nonfiction books, and he strolled by the nonfiction area. The genre didn't please him, and he did not want to enter it. The couch girl was in that section, looking at those books. Circumstances were suddenly different. Eric had to break his own rules and go into the section he despised to talk to the girl.

Eric quickly noticed the girl and went to the aisle where his crush was. He slowed down and walked closer to the girl. Eric stopped and started looking at the books on the shelves.

Andrea turned and looked at the boy. She thought that he was cute. Andrea turned away and kept looking at the books.

Eric looked at her and appreciated her beauty. The girl took a step towards Eric. He turned his head towards her. Andrea turned her head too. They glanced at each other, gave a polite grin, and looked away.

He hated all the books he was staring at. Eric thought the authors were far up their own asses to publish content they thought was correct. His thought was that anyone could be given a pen and paper, but it took a madman to show the world what was inside his head. Eric stepped past the untouchable woman and admired her body.

"So, uh, my friend told me about this book called *Naked Economics*. Have you read it before?" Eric died of anxiety when he opened his mouth. His stomach turned into knots and his heart thumped. After he spoke, a ball of embarrassment sat right behind his throat. Andrea was a little shocked at first and stared at Eric for two aggravating seconds. Eric stood motionless, staring back.

She turned towards Eric and said, "I have, actually. It's a good read if you want a brief understanding of economics."

Eric was confused. He did not know what to do. He did not think it would get this far in his head. He hadn't even read the book. Eric panicked and said, "Cool."

They continued to look at the book titles. Eric thought, *Gah, I'm such an idiot! Why didn't I have a follow up question? Geez, she probably thinks I'm an ass now. She's still standing there and hasn't run out the door, though. I could fix this.*

"My name is Eric. What's your name?"

"Andrea," she said back with a smile.

"Do you go to school or somethin'?"

"I do. I'm a sophomore at UCLA. I'm studying psychology. What about you?"

"Oh, ya know. I'm a car detailer during the day and a starving artist by night."

Eric didn't have the chops to tell her he was only a car washer. Only the best washers were promoted to detailers. But he figured a small lie would not hurt now.

"School just wasn't for me. I always ditched class and never did homework. I got kicked out of my high school for low grades."

Andrea stared at Eric with curiosity.

"But that's how life goes. I'm trying my best to really work on my paintings. Here, you should follow my Instagram." Eric handed her a card that was made from half an index card and displayed his handwritten Instagram handle.

Andrea giggled and took it. "So, was Staples out of ink?" she asked him.

"Oh, nah, I didn't even go there. My sister had index cards when she went to school. I just grabbed a handful. As a matter of fact, some of them have her notes on the back of them." He grabbed the card he had just given to Andrea and flipped it around. She scoffed through her nose. Half a sentence was written in nice penmanship.

"...following, the stigma is what part of the flo..."

"She must've been studying plants," Andrea told Eric. He nodded in agreement and gave her back the card.

Eric felt like he was in trouble. They had nothing in common. He felt he was the opposite of her. But something deep inside was telling him to keep pursuing and not give up. His carnal desires flared up as he stared at the beautiful girl. His mind was hungry to learn more about Andrea.

Andrea was curious about the boy. She did not know if he was lying or telling the truth. There was a mysteriousness about him that drew her closer. She was very attracted to him. The more she looked at his face and physique, the more a light grew inside her. Andrea's hormones spun in circles the longer she talked to Eric. The two strangers talked for five minutes before the conversation tapered off to short responses.

"So, are you originally from L.A.?" Eric asked.

"I've lived here my whole life, especially when I got into the university. It made me love it so much more. I lived in Seattle for a summer for a job. Don't get me wrong; I liked it up there. It was green, and everyone was super friendly. Things moved slower and no one was in a rush. Not like here. You're either wasting someone's time or you're late for something. But L.A. has my heart. I love it."

Eric listened intently. Something struck him when Andrea said the word *love*. It was earnest when she said it. *Love.* She meant it, she felt it, she lived it. His heart beat faster and a warm light shone in his stomach. He wanted her to feel that way about him.

"Wow, sounds like you've lived. I haven't been to too many places, since it's expensive to travel. I've been to Portland and Las Vegas. Once to New York. I would have to agree with you, though. L.A. just has something that other cities can't recreate. Maybe it's Hollywood?"

Andrea chuckled at Eric's joke. Eric smiled back. "I don't want this conversation to stop, but I have to get going pretty soon. I promised my mom I would have dinner with her."

"Isn't that sweet. So your folks live in the area?"

"Close. They grew up in South Central and moved to Whittier."

"Oh, gotcha. Haha, see? Everyone is late for something," she said, smirking at him.

"I guess so. Hey, would you mind if I got your number?" Eric asked.

"Of course."

Eric quickly added her contact to his phone.

"What's your last name?"

"Gomez, Andrea Gomez. Yours?"

"Chavez. I'll text you."

Eric hurried out of the bookshop. Andrea leaned back onto a bookshelf and looked up.

The escape room reminded Eric of when they first met. There was a huge collection of books on one of the walls, and the room smelled of wood and old paper, like a used bookstore. There was a big wooden door with metal braces on the front to prevent it from being opened. It looked like a door that would lead into a castle. But the door had no handle. Upon closer inspection, it had hinges on both sides. It was peculiar, and neither of them had seen anything like it.

"What if they don't want us to leave?" asked Eric.

"To hell with them. I want to leave," Andrea replied.

"Oh, you aren't enjoying it?" he said with disappointment.

"I didn't say that. Some parts were not fun. I was really scared in that last room. I hope they don't do something like that again. But it is interesting. I'll give it that much," Andrea said.

Eric walked over to the door to touch it. He was a very sensory person and thought anything could be analyzed through the senses. Knowledge could be gained through that technique. He looked, but there was no way of opening it.

Andrea noticed a table with a note on it. "Eric, come here; I think I have something," she called. Eric walked over and they looked at the note together. It read:

Here be the lists of ingredients,

Each with its own special power.

Combined, they will show you the true power of complexity.

Follow the instructions as shown and you will witness that power.

1. *Eye of a Doe*

2. *Leg of a Frog*

3. *Salt*

4. *Sweat of a Rabbit*

Put the first two in the boiling cauldron.

Salt after two minutes, not a second more, not a second less.

Garnish with the fourth.

The competence of a chef is needed.

"All those deer we saw had googly eyes. I wonder if there's one without eyes?" Andrea said, making an excellent point.

"We both know I am the better cook between the both of us," Eric said proudly. Andrea agreed. Eric believed cooking took creativity and skill. It was about timing, technique, and style. He loved it because someone could be given a recipe and the list of ingredients, but if the sequence of steps was missing, the dish could not be made correctly. The little nuances made the perfect meal. Sauté the onions until they caramelize; do not grill them. Turn up the heat on high to get the pan hot. Reduce the heat to low and cook the meat perfectly through.

"This clue seems like instructions and not a clue. What do you think it meant by 'each has its own power'?" Eric asked.

"I'm not too keen to figure out how an eyeball can give me powers. I don't want to taste it or feel its texture. I could live the rest of my life happily without experiencing that."

The couple went searching for the items in the room. Andrea went to observe the deer heads.

"The ingredients said 'doe'. I know it can't be one with antlers. Wow, there sure are a lot of deer on this wall," she observed. The wall stretched 25 feet high. The deer heads had something funny about them. All of them had googly eyes. The others were too high to look at. A chair or a ladder could have been really useful to lift her up.

Andrea found a chair, but it was only three feet tall. The next row of deer had googly eyes as well. She let out a deep sigh. There must have been a way to search the ones near the ceiling. A deeper understanding of the building settled in. It was not going to be easy; nothing had been easy so far. Whoever created this place was going to make getting the ingredients a challenge. The correct deer had to be closer to the ceiling. She sat on the chair to think.

Eric walked over to the cauldron. He was curious to know what it looked like on the inside. The fire underneath was hot, and the cauldron was hanging by a metal support. Inside the cauldron was a green vat of liquid. Bubbles rose from the bottom and popped at the surface. It was so thick that the bubbles took time to pop. He looked to see if Andrea was looking at him, but she was too busy observing the deer.

Eric stuck his finger in the cauldron and licked it. The flavor was flat and bitter, but overall, not too bad. The texture was like slime. After tasting the concoction, he felt queasy. His stomach twisted. Eric held onto his stomach and leaned forward.

Eric seemed to fall. Everything pulled away from him. All the objects in the room moved away from him. The cauldron and Eric were the same height.

"Uh oh."

Eric was shrinking! He started patting his body down to see if he could feel the changes happening to him. By the time he started screaming, he was the size of a mouse. His lungs were not big enough to make an audible sound. Eric freaked out. The shoe next to him was the size of a house.

"That's not a good sign."

When Eric looked up from his new perspective, Andrea seemed miles away. Eric yelled for her, but she did not hear one peep.

"What am I gonna do now? I can't please her anymore. There must be a way to get bigger." The table would give him a better vantage point, but it was a mountain compared to him. The chairs towered over him. It would have taken 30 of his body lengths to reach the seat. He could die if he fell off from that height.

There has to be something, he thought. There was a shoelace to sit on and he went into deep thought. Eric scratched his head; he could have really used Andrea's help. He needed to get her attention. Eric thought that setting something on fire would help, but he threw out that idea. *That's stupid! I could set the whole place on fire. One small ember could ignite and spread fast, and this room has no exhaust to the outside. The smoke would eventually suffocate both of us. Huh, I wonder who would die first? She is bigger and can take more smoke. But I'm shorter. I could hide from the smoke the entire time. I am smaller than she is, so it could take less to kill me. I have to figure out how to get off the floor. Hmm, I could draw something. Yeah, that's it, I will make a sign! Brilliant!* Eric leapt off the string to find materials to make a sign for Andrea.

Andrea was still staring at the heads. She wondered if someone killed all the animals, or if they were all fake. Andrea looked for an object to stand on. The room only had chairs. There was no hope of finding a taller object, so she observed the heads in front of her. The googly eyes made her laugh.

Her hand touched the deer's face. It was soft. She ran her fingers through its hair and rubbed up against its cheek. Feeling the dark fur, she knew the deer had a story to tell. It could not speak, but it lived. It ran through the woods, escaped predators, and had a family. The deer spoke to her without speaking. Andrea thought it was a horrific act to murder an animal. She looked at the wall. It was a slaughterhouse. The deer were no competition for lead bullets. They had no protection, no sight of their hunter. One moment they were grazing on the grass, and seconds later, they were bleeding out on the plains.

Andrea cared a little too much. She was a selfless creature; the embodiment of Mother Earth. She cared for Eric greatly and tended to his emotions when he was out of control. She fed his stomach when it trembled. She provided a shoulder to cry on when situations got too tough. Nothing was perfect, but she was the image of perfection in Eric's eyes. Andrea thought of their future together. When she thought of Eric, she started to wonder why he was quiet. He had been too quiet. Eric should have been bothering her and trying to make her laugh with his simple comedy. Andrea was worried.

Andrea could not see him anywhere. Where did he run off to? Nowhere. They were in a closed room.

"Eric!" she yelled out, but got no response. Her stomach sank. Her throat closed. She felt alone. "Quit hiding. This isn't funny." Her voice trembled.

Eric heard her. He yelled back, but she could not hear him. It was a cruel joke. Being close to a loved one but not being able to communicate with them was killing them on the inside. They both had a sinking feeling. They couldn't console each other. It was like a thief stealing from them: one second, they were in each other's possession. Then, suddenly, the other person was the only thing they could think about. When did each one last have their partner? When did they disappear? Who took them? Cui bono? Evil had prevailed and left the couple with questions and sorrow. Someone had stolen Eric from Andrea. Someone had stolen Andrea from Eric.

Eric rushed to gather his materials. He found a couple of pencils and thumbtacks. The pencils were difficult to carry. They were like tree logs. His adrenaline pumped, and with heroic strength, he pulled three pencils from a cup and moved them to the floor. He used those three to make an "H". Eric was proud and happy. A warm sensation went through his body as he thought that his plan would get him out of this mess.

"Things could not get worse, right?" he said. He used the thumbtacks to spell out an "E". While moving the thumbtacks, he pricked his skin. Eric started to bleed a little. But he knew it was worth it. Soon he would be in Andrea's arms.

What would make sense? What could be the easiest way to solve the problem? Eric thought to himself. Eric needed help and he didn't want to lose sight of Andrea.

Andrea paced back and forth, biting her nails. It did not make sense to her. She walked over to the cauldron and saw the green muck inside. It was repulsive. While walking back towards the table, she stepped on some pencils. When she looked down, they looked peculiar. However, when she got closer, she saw all the thumbtacks organized into a nice little "E". She squinted. Andrea got on one knee and looked closer.

It was Eric's chance to get her attention. He darted across the floor and flailed his arms like a madman.

"ANDREA, DOWN HERE!" Eric screamed at the top of his lungs. Andrea looked closer and saw something the size of an ant running across the floor, but it did not look like an ant or move like an ant.

"That's Eric!" She put her hand down quickly and he climbed on her hand like it was a wall of rocks. He plopped down in the middle of her palm. "What did you do?" Andrea asked.

"I wanted to see if the soup in the cauldron was any good, and I gave it a taste. Next thing I knew, everything was getting bigger. I didn't realize I was getting smaller."

"This is a problem. How the hell are we supposed to change you back?"

"I don't know. I was worried you were going to step on me."

"I have you now. That clue said everything has special powers. When we mix them together, their powers are greater. I think we just have to find something that will make you large."

"Yeah, it's a start. I think you're gonna have to do most of the searching for now. It took me like ten minutes to run to the table," Eric said.

"That's fine with me. You should probably just sit back. And don't touch or eat anything else unless we agree on it!" Andrea said sternly.

Andrea started searching the room. The bookshelves were filled with random relics. Everything buzzed, and she was hesitant to touch anything. A reaction could happen to her and the couple would have a smaller chance of getting out. She walked over to the bookcase. There were ancient artifacts like pots, statues, weapons, and weird collectible items. There was a velvet bag with a card next to it that said, *These beans grow.* She thought it was a coincidence. *Jack and the Beanstalk* came to her mind. Maybe if the beans got wet, a giant stalk would grow. It might be possible to climb it and reach the deer at the top.

Andrea picked up the bag and shook the beans into her hand. They felt funny; not like beans. They had a fuzzy feeling to them. Suddenly, she felt the floor shake. Andrea noticed she was as tall as the 10th row of books. Shock overwhelmed her body. When she looked down at the table, it was tiny. Everything around her was getting smaller.

Her height grew at an uncontrollable pace. The ceiling approached and she didn't want to collide with it.

Andrea closed her eyes and waited. Her eyes opened and she was the tallest object in the room. The size of her body was so tremendous that she was scared to move without hitting anything. She was scared that everything would get crushed in her path. However, she could see the top row of deer.

Andrea could use her newfound power to her advantage. All the deer heads were in front of her, and she saw one with real eyes! The eyeball looked squishy and gross. Her hand reached out and grabbed the deer's eye socket. She pushed her finger in. A squishy sound came out, but she had grabbed it!

She wondered how she would shrink. Andrea thought it would be badass to be this tall in the outside world. No one would be bigger than her. They would all respect her because a simple flick of her finger would make them go flying.

Something changed inside of Andrea. Her vision got blurry, so she rubbed her eyes, but it seemed to get worse. Darkness flooded the corners of her eyes. Moments later, she was completely blind. Andrea freaked out and started screaming. Eric quickly covered his ears because she sounded like a fire alarm.

"Am I blind?" Andrea stuck out her arm and collided with the bookcase and the deer heads. She was stunned. Her blurry vision could not make out any of the shapes.

"This is not good at all." Andrea stood there like a statue. She didn't know what to do next.

If I'm huge and Eric's small, I just have to do what Eric did to get small. What did he say he did? Ah, he licked the potion in the cauldron! It would be difficult to get to the cauldron without her vision. It annoyed her that she could not sit down. She rubbed her chin while she thought.

Andrea boiled it down to her senses. Her senses consisted of taste, smell, hearing, and touch. Vision was useless for her current situation. Andrea thought about touching the deer heads again. That idea got the wheels turning in her head.

She could use her hand to feel the warmth of the cauldron. She bent down slowly and started waving her hand like a metal detector. At first, she felt nothing. She wondered why. Andrea forgot how tall she was, and she couldn't see the floor.

The floor had to be near her feet. Her hand moved closer to the floor and touched her knee. *Hmm, just a little farther,* she thought. The tips of her fingers could feel her ankle. Her ankle was close, so she went a bit lower. She found the floor.

"Ha!" she called out. Andrea started patting the floor. She heard a noise. *Tsss.*

Her hand immediately pulled back, and she sucked on her finger. "Even though I'm much bigger, hot is still hot," Andrea said.

She stuck her finger in her mouth and sucked. The cauldron had burned her finger, but she knew where the cauldron was. Andrea reached down to the same location and felt for the warmth. She located the edges of the cauldron. She dipped her fingers in and got them wet. There was soup on her fingers, and she licked it.

"Whoa, that tastes rancid," she said.

Immediately, the effects started to take over. Andrea didn't know if she was shrinking because her vision didn't come back. Her hands flailed side to side. Her surroundings could be anywhere. She didn't hit any deer heads. When she took a step forward, she did not come into contact with anything. Andrea didn't know where she was going.

A table hit her hips. Andrea was excited that she was back to her original height, but the lack of vision made her fearful.

"Hey, Eric, I don't know where you're at, but I'm blind now," Andrea yelled.

"Huh, what do you mean?"

"What?"

"I said, what do you mean!"

"Damn, I can barely hear you!"

"WALK CLOSER TO ME!" Eric yelled back.

"I'm going to walk around. Just say stuff so I can figure out where you're at," Andrea replied.

"Eggs and bacon. Eggs and bacon. Eggs and bacon!"

Eric was so small that Andrea could not hear what he said. There was no way for Andrea to see next to her, so she stuck out her arms to feel around. There was a possibility she could run into a wall. Sometimes she could hear Eric, but she always lost track of where his voice was coming from. Her hearing was the only sense she could rely on, and she felt like a bat going into a cave. A high-pitched scream came from the ground. She immediately stopped and looked around. There was something by her foot. She bent down and figured out what the noise was.

"Hey, down here, you big boof! Put your hand on the floor!" Eric yelled.

"Who are you calling 'boof'? Why would I help you now?" Andrea retorted.

Eric stayed quiet. The guilt got to the best of Andrea, and she put her hand down. Eric started to climb up her hand. The creases in Andrea's hands allowed him to climb up. He finally plopped down, and she lifted him up to the table. Andrea tilted her hand downwards. Eric lost his footing and jumped down. He toppled down and landed on his ass.

"Hey, you gotta be more careful with me. If I fall a couple inches, that's a couple feet for me. If I jumped off this table, I'd splatter like a cake."

"Eric, I'm blind. I can't see shit."

"Wait, what? When did that happen?"

"Right after I grabbed the doe's eye. Everything started getting fuzzy and blurry. Black creeped in, and then nothing. It's like looking at a TV that has no signal. Everything is blurry, and I can't see what anything is. It's horrible. I'm terribly scared," Andrea said.

Eric heard the tremor in her voice and started to get concerned. "I'm sure we can figure this out, Andrea. If you were able to get big and back to normal, I can get bigger and help you get your vision back. Wait, how did you grow in the first place?" Eric asked.

"I grabbed some stupid beans from the shelves. After that I shot up straight towards the ceiling," Andrea said.

"Huh. Do you have them with you?" Eric asked.

"No, I put them back down. They're probably still there. Oh, I see what you're getting at. You need those beans now," Andrea said.

"Exactly! But how are you going to find something when you're blind? Why don't you grab me and put me on your shoulder? I can talk into your ear and be your eyes."

"That's actually a pretty good idea."

"Finally!" Eric cheered.

The two worked as a strong team. Andrea's hand went down onto the table and Eric began to climb. Eric began to struggle, but Andrea gave him a boost up. Eric walked into the palm of her hand. She grabbed him and brought him all the way up. Andrea moved her hand quickly and Eric fell to his butt. He chuckled, saw a shoulder to climb on, and grabbed onto her shirt to pull himself up. Finally, he maintained his balance and grabbed onto Andrea's earlobe.

"Hey, all good?" Eric asked.

"Yeah, I feel funny. I feel like I'm sleeping. But I'm sure we can get through it," Andrea responded.

"Do you remember what the bookcase looked like? There's a couple in this room. There are two tall ones. They stretch to the ceiling. And there are four other ones that are probably close to eight feet tall."

"Hmm... I know I didn't reach high for it. But what was in the bookcase is all fuzzy in my memory. I just remember shooting up. But the deer were close by. That's how I was able to get the eye."

Eric looked for the deer. While he searched, he noticed the deer on one wall, and saw two bookcases nearby. Either bookcase may have had the beans.

"There's only two of 'em. I say we go with the taller one first. That one got your attention," Eric said.

"Okay, lead the way, Captain," Andrea responded.

"Alright. Turn ninety degrees to the right," Eric instructed Andrea. She went in the opposite direction.

"Okay, good. Now I want you to go to your left just a tad. Rotate. Do not walk anywhere." Andrea turned in the right direction this time. The bookcase was not far.

"Perfect. Do the same thing you just did!"

Andrea turned, but she overshot the direction. Eric was getting frustrated.

"Okay, close. Go the opposite direction you just went, but less."

"We need to figure out a new system. I have no idea what you are talking about. Can you use a clock?"

"There's no clocks in here," Eric stated.

"Ugh, you idiot. Like, tell me 'three o'clock, six o'clock, nine o'clock'. That way I know how far and the direction."

"Oh, I get you. Let me see. Okay, for the big bookshelf, turn to nine o'clock." Andrea turned. She slowed her movements and aimed for nine with her toes. She smirked knowing she was right, but she knew Eric would never admit it.

"Perfect! Okay, take about five paces forward now. Okay, good. You're about three steps away. Just stick out your hand. Walk slowly and closer towards that direction." Andrea walked closer with tiny steps.

"Closer, closer, closer, you're almost there!"

Andrea's hand bumped into the wall, and she stopped.

"What do you see, Eric?" she asked.

"I see a bunch of books. It looks like some plants, maybe a pothos nearby. I see a typewriter, a little doll, and a Newton's cradle, I think. Hey, what did the beans look like? Were they in anything?"

"Let me think. Yeah, they were in a little bag. It was soft. I don't remember the color, though." Eric scanned each shelf. He looked for a bag, but found nothing. He kept looking. The shelf had earthy tones. A.J. had loved nature, so he incorporated it into many of his rooms. Some figurines on the shelves had his initials inscribed at the bottom. Eric thought the beans may be close by because of all the plants.

"I'm not seeing anything. We may have to go to the other bookcase."

"Okay, I trust you. Let's do it."

"Okay, turn to your three o'clock." Andrea turned just the way Eric asked.

"Now take six steps towards that direction. Stop, and let's see how far you get." Andrea took her steps while Eric analyzed the area.

"Alright, now take three more steps and stop.Turn back to twelve o'clock. You are right in front of the bookcase. Stick out your hand to feel the shelf. It's right there."

Slowly, Andrea felt the shelf.

"Okay, take a couple steps back. I want to see the whole thing."

Andrea stepped back and Eric was able to get a better perspective on the shelf. He looked at the bottom shelf first, but only saw books. The second shelf had more books, but there was a figurine of a person as well.

The figurine was a wooden man with moveable joints for an artist to draw. The wooden man had a small *A.J.* written at the top of his foot. Eric shook his head and looked at the third shelf. Another figurine was a very curvy statue that looked old. It resembled a woman. But he did not see any bags. Next to the statue was a broken plate with gold in the cracks to make the plate a whole piece. Once broken, the plate was put back together with the Japanese art of kintsugi.

He looked at the shelf above and noticed strange, ancient artifacts. Finally, he could see the velvet bag that they had been searching for.

"Hey, can you take a few steps forward? I think I see something. It's a small bag."

Andrea took a few steps forward. "I don't want to touch that thing again. It was horrible," Andrea said.

"How do you want to do it? I can run across your arm like a bridge."

"Absolutely not! What if you fall? I can grab you and place you on the shelf."

"I don't feel too comfortable with that," Eric said sternly.

"Are you scared it would hurt your macho-ness? Being handled by a woman?" The tone in her voice changed, and she smiled as she said it. Eric stayed quiet.

"I like my bridge idea," he said with a firm voice.

"I'm not doing it. I'm not going to risk your life if there's a safer option."

Eric sat on her shoulder and thought.

"Fine. Just be careful with me. Don't grab me. I'll just crawl into your hand. Don't grab me by my clothes."

Andrea chuckled and laid her hand down for Eric to climb onto. Andrea made sure to keep him level. Her knuckles touched the shelf and her hand opened. Eric ran off the tip of her finger and jumped to the shelf. He stumbled when he landed and regained his balance. Eric looked for the bag and saw it to the right of him. A note caught his attention. It said, *These beans grow.* Eric opened the velvet bag and walked inside. The beans were stacked inside the bag. The beans were bigger than his head. Eric grabbed a bean and started getting a funny feeling. Something was tingling and he was growing!

He grew more quickly than anticipated. The top shelf got closer to his head. He held up his hands before he came into contact with the top. Thump! The shelf knocked him down and he fell to the ground. The fall didn't hurt him. Eric knocked the shelf over and all the artifacts came rolling down. They hit him in the stomach, one by one.

"Damn, that hurt! Everything landed on my stomach!"

Andrea didn't know what had happened, but giggled at Eric's pain.

"What happened? Are you okay? Did you grow?" Andrea asked sincerely.

"Yeah. Too fast. I hit my head on the shelf! Everything came toppling down on me!"

Andrea smiled. "I wish I could've seen it."

Eric rolled his eyes and asked, "So, what items do we have?"

"We have the eye of the doe. That's the one that made me blind. I don't think I can be of any help with this condition," Andrea said.

"That's fine, I can be your eyes. If I do get stuck with something, I'll come ask you."

They agreed on the plan. Eric pulled up a chair and asked Andrea to sit. It was possible she could have hurt herself by walking into something dangerous. He was able to sit her down on a chair. Eric was weirded out by her stare. Her face was blank and empty as she looked towards a wall. Andrea was left only with her thoughts, and nothing else. Everything was dark and unclear. She stared into the void and it made her stomach uneasy.

Eric walked over to the bookcase with the beans. There were only artifacts on it.

"Hmm. Leg of a frog, salt, and sweat of a rabbit."

There was nothing in the bookcase. Next to the cauldron, there were shelves with hundreds of vials. The vials all had names on them.

"Fairy dust, sweat of a dog, brain poison, enchanted vial, and so on. One of them has to be here," Eric read out.

Eric kept looking, and on the third shelf, he saw a vial labeled *salt*.

"Whoa!" he quickly grabbed it off the shelf. The vial had tiny white crystals on the inside. He shook all the grains around in a swirl. The salt could have had weird after-effects, but he contemplated tasting it. Eric grabbed the vial and put it on the table. "I found the salt!" he said.

"How do you know it's salt?" Andrea responded.

"Well, it's labeled," Eric said.

"I don't trust anything in the place. But you know what? Let me test it. I'm already blind. It's best if we don't lose the only good person on the team," Andrea said.

"Yeah, that's true. I will put it on the table. Let me move your hand on top so you know where it's at." He moved her hand on top of the shaker. She felt the shaker, shook the salt into her hand, and tasted it.

"It's salty. Let's give it some time." Andrea put it back on the wooden table along with the doe's eye. She cautioned Eric not to touch the eye.

"Time to go back to searching," Eric said. He left the table and looked around the room. The room was old and Victorian. All of the furniture was wooden and intricate. There were paintings that looked very old, and candle holders lined the wall. The rug and drapes were distasteful in Eric's opinion. They had flashy patterns and deep color schemes.

The walls had drapes covering windows. Behind the windows were bricks. They were completely blocked off. Eric was disappointed: he had hoped for sunlight. While he looked in that spot, he noticed something in the corner. There was a little white bunny trembling. He recognized it; it was the same bunny from the field of roses around the lake.

"Hey there buddy. It's going to be okay." His hand reached out for the bunny, but the animal took off with the swiftness of a shooting star. Eric tried to follow, but it disappeared somewhere in the room.

There was a puddle where the bunny stood. Eric was hesitant to find out if it was sweat or pee. A cloth napkin was on the table next to him. Eric grabbed the napkin and soaked the cloth in the liquid. Once the liquid was on the napkin, he smelled it. Nothing putrid. They had the sweat of a rabbit. He put the napkin in his pocket and returned to Andrea.

"You're not gonna believe it! I found the rabbit that we saw earlier. He's a spastic fellow. When I walked closer, the rabbit's eyes grew wide. He started shivering and then booked it! I was shocked. He left a puddle behind him. I soaked a napkin in it. I'm pretty sure it's the sweat."

"That's fantastic! Hopefully you didn't grab piss."

They both chuckled.

The last item they needed was the leg of a frog. They were stuck on how to find it quickly. Eric started to pace the room, which allowed him to think better. Eric's pace picked up.

He cleared several bookcases in less than a second. He noticed he could reach the other end of the room in half a second. Andrea sat, blindly staring at a wall. Her gaze was daunting. Her mind buzzed, but without any visual stimulation. Eric looked at his watch.

The second hand was at three o'clock, and he memorized its position. He dashed across the room and looked back at his watch. The second hand was in the same spot. While gazing a little longer, he saw that it finally ticked. Eric was in awe. A couple seconds later, Andrea called out.

"Why the hell are you running in here?"

He chuckled and decided to play a trick on her.

Every two seconds, he touched her nose. In the middle of a second, he ran back to the other side of the room.

"I'm over here!" Eric called out. He ran over to Andrea and back.

"Whoa! Something touched my nose!" Andrea yelped.

"What do you mean?" Eric ran over again, touched her nose, and quickly darted back.

"Ah, there it is again!" she shrieked.

"What are you freaking out about? I don't see anything. Hold on, let me go to you." He walked a little closer, but went really slowly. When he was halfway to her, he touched her nose one last time.

"What the fuck is in front of me, Eric?" She was clearly scared. Eric finally approached her more slowly.

"Oh wow, you won't believe it. I'm super fast. I can run across this room a thousand times, but when I look at the clock, it only moves a couple seconds."

Andrea sat there with a puzzled look. "I don't understand, how are you that fast? Are you messing with me? You realize I can't see anything."

"I know, I'm sorry. It was me touching your nose! I can run to you in less than a second."

"Whoa, impressive. It must've been from the rabbit sweat!" Andrea said.

"Yeah, no kidding. Damn, looks like you pulled the short straw."

"I have nothing to say to you," Andrea said with spite.

"I could probably look for everything a lot faster now," Eric replied.

"That is true. Get searching, kid," Andrea said with attitude.

Eric scoffed and started scouring the shelves. Within seconds he came back to Andrea.

"Okay, I'm done. I looked through everything."

"That was only three seconds."

"I know, I move in milliseconds. It's great. I found the leg of a frog in a jar! I also found this. It's called 'vision potion'. It didn't say anything else on the label. Do you think it could work for you?"

"Hm, I guess it's worth a shot. It's better than nothing."

Eric handed over the potion. Andrea rubbed it on her hands. Nothing happened. She was disappointed, and figured it was a drink. She dipped her finger in and licked it.

Moments passed, and Andrea felt defeated. Slowly, shades of beige started filling her vision. Everything was a complete blur, but a bit of light reached her eyes. She grabbed the bottle again and took a full swig. It did not taste bad. Her vision was returning. The blurriness changed into shapes. Color came back, and lines became apparent to Andrea.

"I'm starting to see again! Things are a tad blurry, but it's definitely coming back to focus!"

"That's amazing! Oh my god, I'm really glad," Eric said.

Andrea sat and waited for her full eyesight to come back. Eric prepared the ingredients on the table. He made the fire hotter by adding wood and fanning the flames. They needed the cauldron to be at a full boil. Andrea finally got her vision back. She ran behind Eric and gave him a tight hug. He smiled and hugged her back. The couple looked into each other's eyes and pecked each other on the lips.

"I started getting everything ready. But hold on - check this out. Look at the little nightstand. Nothing, right? I want you to look at my watch, and right when it strikes the twelve, wait one second and look back at the nightstand," Eric said.

She nodded her head, looked at the clock and turned around to the nightstand. Andrea gasped. A tiny pyramid made of little logs appeared in less than a second. She turned to Eric and smiled. He chuckled and said he told her so.

The cauldron was at a full boil. Eric grabbed the recipe and read it again.

Follow the instructions as shown and you will witness that power.

1. *Eye of a Doe*

2. *Leg of a Frog*

3. *Salt*

4. *Sweat of a Rabbit*

Put the first two in the boiling cauldron.

Salt after two minutes, not a second more, not a second less.

Garnish with the fourth.

"Okay, I will do the first part. We will both keep time, but you do the salt. It must be precise timing, and you're the man to do it," Andrea said.

Eric agreed. Andrea put the first two ingredients in. They splashed and floated to the top. She picked up a ladle and started to stir. They both stared into the sauce. After a minute, the two ingredients started to vanish and changed the color of the soup from green to orange. The two-minute mark was coming up, and Eric had the salt ready in his hand.

"How much do I put?" Eric asked.

"Just a couple shakes. No one likes salty food," Andrea responded.

The minute hand struck the top of the watch face and Eric started to add the salt. They let it cook and boil a little longer. The vat of sauce became less viscous and more of a watery texture.

"I think it's ready," Andrea said. She grabbed two clay mugs and poured a scoopful in each. She set them down on the table. Eric grabbed the napkin and dipped it into their drink. The drink became purple after the sweat was added. They looked at each other and shrugged their shoulders. They each grabbed a cup and clinked them.

"Down the hatch," Eric said.

"Bottoms up," Andrea replied.

The couple chugged their concoction. They smacked their lips after finishing. It was actually pretty good, and sweet to the palette.

"Feel any different?" Eric asked.

"Not too much. But it was sweet."

They sat and waited. Andrea observed her surroundings and saw a faint, rectangular glow on one of the walls. She proceeded to walk towards it. Eric noticed the same glow and looked at the wall.

"What do you think it is?" Eric asked.

"Hopefully our way out," Andrea responded.

Eric stuck out his hand to touch the wall, but missed it. He was confused. His hand didn't contact anything.

There was no sensation in his hand. He reached out, and the same thing happened. Andrea looked at Eric and saw his hand go through the wall!

"Whoa, your hand went through the wall."

Eric was shocked. "You try it now."

Andrea stuck her hand into the wall. Eric was in awe.

"You were right! We found our way out." They grabbed each other's hands and walked through the wall together.

CHAPTER 4: FLOAT

Andrea and Eric stepped through the wall. It took them to a different room. The room had furniture on the ceiling. A ceiling fan was on the floor. The door was at the top and an exit sign was at the bottom.

"It did say it would give us powers," Andrea exclaimed. Eric tried jumping, but nothing happened. He laid on the floor and looked up. Nothing fell on top of the couple. Eric and Andrea were oriented the wrong way. The room was upside down. They walked on the ceiling. Eric ran around the room, and he noticed his super speed was still active. Andrea gave him a thumbs up.

They noticed a countertop with a small window that was right-side up compared to the rest of the room. It was a teller's window. They walked over and saw a bell, and Eric pressed it. *Ding!* The couple expected a person to come out. A small door opened in the window glass. A conveyor belt rolled out two drinks. They were glass milkshake cups with red and white straws. They had a brown liquid at the bottom, ice cream, and whipped cream on top. Eric grabbed one and started drinking. Andrea hesitated.

"Whoa, that's great!"

Eric finished the drink. Andrea stared at him gently. She noticed his head was getting a little higher. She looked down and his feet were off the ground.

"You're floating!"

"Whoa! Check me out - I'm levitating, and no strings attached! I think it's this drink. It tastes like root beer," Eric said in the air.

"Let me try." Andrea took a sip and her eyes opened wide. "It's a root beer float!"

Eric tried to put down the empty glass, but had difficulty. He tried to maintain his balance in the air, but always fell forward and did somersaults. It was way too difficult to stand on air. Lying down seemed like the better option. He stared at Andrea, admiring her. She floated perfectly still with her hands waving up and down.

Andrea adjusted much more quickly than Eric. She started to twirl with one knee bent and her hands pointed straight up. When she flapped her arms, her body flew up into the air. When her hands pointed down, she drifted closer to the floor. Eric tried to spin, but he found himself in a loop. He barrel rolled and couldn't slow down. The momentum would keep him spinning forever. His spins got faster and faster. Andrea flew to him and laid her hand on his shoulder to stop his spinning. She pulled him to the side.

"Concentrate and focus all of your energy on one thing. Harness it, use it, own it. Try staring at that vase in the top corner, the one with zigzags."

Eric squinted at the vase. He tried to feel the object with his eyes and stared hard.

"Try going up now," Andrea told him.

Eric focused on flying upwards. He started to float up.

"I'm doing it!" he shouted out. Andrea flew circles around Eric until he found his balance. However, he fell in the air and hit his butt on nothing. Andrea laughed at him, but helped him get back up. Andrea started to glide across the room with ease, observing everything, while Eric tried to get his bearings.

Andrea swept Eric off his feet. He looked up at her in a trance. She was confident in her abilities. Eric was in awe. He looked up at her as they flew around the room. She looked down at him, and happiness beamed from her eyes.

"You're getting really good at this. I don't know how you're able to coordinate so well with the space around you," Eric told Andrea.

"Yeah, I am not too sure. It came naturally. Once I adjusted how my body spins, it got pretty easy." Eric heard what she said and thought about it. She got closer to the ground and dropped him off. Once she let go, she did a backflip in the air to celebrate.

Andrea noticed a banner that hung upside down, and she floated sideways to read the sign.

Go on and float, just don't rock the boat.

Interesting, she thought to herself.

"Hey Eric, when you get a chance, can you come over here to read this with me?" Andrea asked.

"Yep, I'll be right there." He took longer than she expected. Andrea turned and saw that he was tiptoeing his way there. "That's a cool sign. Think it can help us?" Eric said.

"I am sure," Andrea said.

They looked together, but couldn't find the boat anywhere. They thought about how a boat could be useful in their situation. It looked like a normal room: some seats, lamps, desks, and paintings. Eric sat on the couch that was stuck to the ceiling and Andrea walked in circles with her feet above the ground. A voice came overhead and asked if they wanted a hint.

"Will there be something taken in return?" Andrea asked.

"Who knows," the machine responded. They looked at each other and said yes.

"The painting reveals a story."

The couple took the hint and started to look at the paintings. All of them seemed normal except one. It was wrapped around a gold wooden frame. It appeared to be old. It was a picture of an old dock where boats were tied up. People walked on the boardwalk and birds chased each other. They kept looking until Eric finally figured out what was odd about it. The water moved in the painting.

"Look at the water! It's rippling. It could be one of those video paintings."

He put his head closer and heard bells ringing, people murmuring, and birds squawking in the distance. "Do you hear that, Andrea?"

"Yeah, I do. Is it coming from the painting?"

"I believe so."

Eric stuck out his hand toward the painting and saw it shake and grow smaller. He started to get scared and pulled back. "Whoa! Did you see that? It started to pull me in. Hm, okay. I don't want to do this alone. Let's hold hands?"

Andrea accepted. This time the couple did it together at once. Their hands began to shrink, and a force started to pull the couple towards the painting. The painting sucked Eric and Andrea into the frame. They fell deeper and deeper. They turned into tiny people and fell through the air!

They gained speed. The couple flipped and saw water beneath them. They pulled up before they made an impact. They floated above the water and looked at each other.

"Hey, is my vision going out? You look funny," Eric asked.

"Whoa, so do you. You're like a poor oil painting of yourself," Andrea replied.

"Yeah, no kidding. It's blurry, but I can make out that you're a person. And this water looks like shit," Eric said.

"Yeah, it's like we're in a different dimension. I have no idea what this is."

The couple adjusted to their new reality. Nothing was defined or had crisp edges. Eric looked closer at Andrea, and the detail started to pop out on her.

"Oh my gosh, what are you wearing?" Eric couldn't contain his laughter. He burst out with a howl. Andrea grabbed her dress and looked at it.

"My, it's hideous. You're right. I wouldn't be caught dead in this thing. But I'm no joke compared to you. Look at what you're wearing," Andrea retorted.

Eric looked down and saw the awful moss-green clothing. White ruffles flowed out of his collar and down to his pants.

"I think I'm gonna be sick. Okay, let's figure this out," Eric stated.

"Touch the water," Andrea said.

"The water feels like water. My finger got wet when I dunked it in," Eric said.

"Whoa, check it out, I can move the water with my hands!" Andrea formed a tentacle with the water and wiggled it everywhere. Andrea started to imagine the capabilities of her new power. She gently floated down and sat inches above the water. The water started to move underneath her. A splash of water rose up and formed a wall. All of the water splashed back down to the ocean. Andrea stood up on her newly formed platform.

"Hey, come stand on my boat," said Andrea. Eric was intrigued. He slowly lowered himself with his arms flailing.

"Whoa, finally. Solid ground." Eric tried to look at what he was standing on, but the boat was invisible to both of them. He walked on the boat, but knocked his face into a pole he couldn't see. He rubbed his nose.

"I guess we oughta head over to that small town over there," Eric said.

Andrea took a closer look and agreed. They raised the sails and started en route to the port.

They were parking the boat when a gentleman with a British accent walked up to them and said, "Nice boat you got there, chap. Welcome to the Port of London. To what kind of business do you attend here?"

"Um, thanks, just got her up and running not too long ago. But we are here because we are traders... You know, small things and oddities."

"Peculiar. Please pay the dock fee and feel free to leave your boat parked in the harbor. It is due north about two kilometers. There you can find bedding, food, and a cup of tea. Thank you, and have a merry day." He tipped his hat and walked away.

The attendant said under his breath, "What peculiar accents they have."

"Alright, let's set the direction and head to the harbor. I'm starving!" Eric said.

They set sail for their new destination. The couple couldn't believe the situation they were in. They had never felt more connected as they explored new lands with each other, sailing across the ocean to a bizarre new world. They looked back at each other and smiled. Eric thought of how the craziness started, with one door opening. Andrea thought about how grateful she was to have someone like Eric, who was always taking them on adventures. She was lovestruck. And Eric was always off in his own world, letting his fascinations take him. But Andrea knew that Eric cared for her deeply.

"Hey, you wanna do the *Titanic* pose?" Eric asked. Andrea broke away from her daydream and laughed. She ran over and stood in front of Eric. He pushed up against her back and grabbed her hands. He lifted them up, and they could feel the sea breeze hitting their faces.

"I'M ON A BOAT!" Eric shouted.

Andrea shook her head. "That's the phrase you want? Not 'I'm king of the world?'" Andrea asked.

"Wait, who says that?" Eric asked.

Andrea rolled her eyes. "Jack! From *Titanic?*"

"Oh yeah, I forgot he said anything. And besides, why would I want to be a king? That's so much responsibility. How would I feed a country if I can't even feed myself cereal in the morning?"

Andrea loosened her grasp, and when Eric noticed, he gave her a big bear hug, kissed her on the cheek, and let her go. Eric put his arms out as if he were looking through a telescope.

"Yep, there it is, right about there. Yea, right there. That's the harbor the man told us about." Faint glowing lanterns appeared with music and people jabbering. They were able to find a spot for their boat. The couple jumped down and started walking towards the land. Another gentleman walked up to them. He had the same face as the other dock attendant.

"Hey, weren't you at that other place we parked? By the docks?" Eric asked.

"I was most certainly not. I am here in front of you, at the harbor. How can I help you?" said the man with the same British accent.

"We're looking to park our boat. We're traders and we're looking for a place to crash and get food."

"Well, I... please do not crash your boat. There are rules here. As far as food, you may go up Main Street. You can find lodging and public houses along the way. Now for your fee: it'll be thirty quid to leave the boat. Seventy quid to park it overnight. You will be charged the King's Tax. Do you know how long you will be staying with us, sir?"

"Uh, you know. Maybe two or four."

"Two or four what, sir?

"Hell, maybe even seven."

The attendant looked confused.

"We're going to be here for a couple hours," Andrea said.

"Excuse me, fair lady, but I was talking to your husband. Not you."

"Whoa, rude. But yeah, a couple of hours. If we aren't gone by sundown you can bill us in the morning."

"Thank you. Your total is sixty-five quid."

"That is outlandish, highway robbery! Won't you go any lower?" Eric started to bargain. "Look. My wife and I are out of town, trying to get back home to our parents and children. We will not be long."

"I am sorry, sir, but that is the price. No exceptions."

"You see, I'm a merchant. How about I give you this really nice pen? Could that lower the price?" Eric stuck out his hand as if he were holding a pen, but nothing was there.

"That is a very elegant-looking pen. Fine. Sixty quid."

"Deal." He shook the man's hand and handed over the invisible pen.

"Ahem, tipping is expected," said the attendant.

"Sure, man. It's in this bag. Keep the other five for yourself."

Eric tossed him an imaginary bag. The attendant reached out and caught it. He had a surprised look on his face due to the young man's manners.

Eric grabbed Andrea by the side and walked toward the shore. He lifted his hand up and clicked imaginary keys to make sure their boat was safe.

"Hey, how'd you do that?" Andrea asked.

"I figured if you could think of a boat, I can think of objects. So, I decided to make a pen and money. It was easy. I just felt like the pen was in my hand. He saw it and believed it. Or everyone here is just gullible."

Andrea wanted to practice, but Eric said to leave it and find a place to rest first. They were walking on the pier when they noticed a flyer nailed into a wooden post. It read, *WANTED: witches and the like. Anyone who gets seen casting magic will skip trial and be burned at the stake. 200 quid reward.*

"Looks like we have to be careful when floating or making objects. They might think we're witches," Andrea said.

"You're my main witch," Eric said with a stern tone and flirtatious eyes. Andrea scoffed at him.

The couple arrived at the boardwalk and noticed what everyone wore. There were high-class jackets with big buttons, tight leggings and uncomfortable black shoes. The girls were in big puffy dresses with tight corsets in the middle, giving them a distinct hourglass shape.

"If you ask me, there are way too many frills on clothing here," Eric said to Andrea.

"I totally see what you mean. Look at that lady over there. That one with the mint dress and her hair high in a pink bow. She has ruffles on her dress, sleeves, neckline, everywhere! Even her hair has curls in it," Andrea exclaimed.

"They say fashion repeats itself. I'm sure glad they left this trend behind."

They had a good laugh together. A sign that read *INN* was on the side of a brickwork building. A slight drizzle started to fall on them. They walked at a brisk pace towards the lodge. The door hit a bell as soon as they entered. Inside was a man behind a reception desk reading a newspaper and holding a pipe. A cup of tea was next to him. His face was long and pale, while his eyes were sunken in. His voice was long.

"Hellooo, welcome to the Innnn. I am here if you need assistance."

"Hi, I was wondering if I could get a room here?" Eric asked. The man looked up at him. He criticized Eric with his eyes. The receptionist let out a deep sigh, sipped his tea, and turned.

"Let me seeee if I have vacancy." Eric and Andrea could see keys hanging on a pegboard behind the grumpy man. They noticed one was missing. The man stared until, finally, he turned around. He looked at them both, scanning. He gave them another long stare. "Yes, we have rooooooooms available. People come later at night after time in the public house, so I suggessst you get it now."

Eric nodded in agreement.

"Goood, goood. Nice head on those shoulders. Here is your room key for one-B. It's down the hall and three doors to your right. I will be here until ten p.m., and then it's lights out. I don't come back until eight a.m. Any complaints after ten will have to be voiced in the morning. If urgent matters require, you can always go to the police department down the streeeet. Now if you'll excuse me, I have my reading to attend tooooo," he said, picking up his newspaper. Eric grabbed the key and said thank you. The couple walked to their room.

"That was an odd fellow," Eric observed.

Andrea agreed with Eric. They entered their room and laid on the bed. They were exhausted. They took a nap, showered, and got ready. They left the room, locked the door, and walked to the street.

The sun was setting and beams of light peeked out and illuminated the streets. They looked out and saw police patrolling the night as it got darker. Street hustlers tried to make a quick buck off small trinkets. A drunken crowd was rowdy close by. Music came from the public house, along with cheerful laughs and conversation. It looked like the right place for the couple. They walked towards the pub. The voices, the excitement, and the energy coming from inside were pulsating.

The couple enjoyed hearing the chatter of people, even though the people looked like paintings. Eric sat down at the bar and grabbed the bartender's attention.

"Excuse me, can I get two fish and chips and two beers?"

The bartender didn't say anything back, but nodded his head in acknowledgement. He brought over two warm beers. Eric and Andrea picked them up and cheered each other. They were taken aback by the taste of warm beer.

"That's not the best beer, but at least the taste is there," Eric said.

"I don't know. I think you can finish mine," replied Andrea. Eric shrugged and took the beer. Their food came and they scarfed down what was in front of them. They couldn't remember the last time they had eaten. The couple felt rejuvenated after they ate and drank. All of the escape rooms were wearing them out.

They couldn't talk about their powers with anyone because no one would understand. Or worse: the couple would be accused of performing magic.

An older gentleman approached the couple. "'Ello there you two, what brings you to this side of town?" the stranger asked.

Eric replied, "Oh, we're traders just passing through. We're waiting 'til morning to start sailing again."

"Interesting; you do not look like much of a sea traveler."

"You bet. We have a nice ship. We sell trinkets and collectibles. Would you be interested?"

"You do have my attention if you are a salesman that can afford a boat."

Eric reached into his coat pocket. He stuck out his hand, but nothing was in it.

"Here is a vintage stopwatch. It'll make sure you always keep time and are never late. How much would you pay for this?"

The man hesitated.

"I would assume no more than fifty quid."

Eric acted shocked. "Nonsense! A timepiece like this goes for one hundred! I want you to notice the hand-carved intricacies. It takes a master craftsman to make something of this value."

Eric handed over the fictitious watch. The man observed it, bringing it close to his eyes, feeling the weight, and looking at the secondhand move. He didn't acknowledge Andrea at all. She continued eating her meal.

"Ah, I now see the skill that went into making this watch. It sure is a fine watch."

"I have had a good trip selling off my inventory. How about I do eighty quid for you?"

"I'm sorry chap. The highest I can do is seventy quid, as that's all I have on me."

"Deal."

Eric and the man shook hands and made the exchange.

"Andrea, look, real money. Now we can pay the hotel fee just fine."

"Good job. I didn't know you had a bargainer and salesman in you."

"I guess I am adapting to my surroundings. Hey, let's go to the tables so we don't get weirdos talking to us at the bar."

Andrea nodded in agreement and went to a table that was private.

"What else do you think you can do with your new powers?" Andrea asked.

"I don't know. I feel like anything I can imagine will come to fruition. Can you see the things I create?" Eric asked.

"Unfortunately, no. They only fool the people that exist in this painting."

Eric started to think while he finished his meal. He started to get a bit buzzed from the beer.

"I have an idea! Let me make a change holder."

Eric waved his hands in the air and thought of the change holder. He grabbed the money and put it inside. Meanwhile, the man at the bar observed the couple. His eyes grew wide when he saw the bag appear from nowhere. He finished his drink, slammed it down, and ran outside.

"How long do you want to stay here?" Eric asked.

"Let's get some rest and wait 'til morning to leave," Andrea responded.

"I like that idea."

The couple was clearing the table when suddenly, four policemen came into the bar with the same man who had bought the watch from Eric.

"That's them! In the corner! I saw them perform magic - it's witchcraft, I tell you! Witchcraft!"

The police locked eyes with the couple and walked towards them.

"Fuck, what should we do?" Andrea asked.

"I think we should just let them take us. We have no family, lawyer, or support."

"Excuse me, this man here claims you are performing magic. That crime is punishable by death. We are going to have to take you in for questioning. We're going to lock you both up until we get this cleared or you get a sentence. Please stand and place your hands behind your backs while my partners apply hand restraints."

The couple complied; worry flowed through their bones. Andrea looked at Eric for comfort, but Eric only returned a look of sadness. The cops grabbed the two and started to push them out the door. They walked down the street. The jailhouse was not far from the public house. Andrea held her head down in shame. Her hair covered her face. Even though no one knew her, strangers' judgmental eyes pierced through the locks of her hair.

Eric wondered how he would escape. He saw a promising alley that was dimly lit and had many exits. His best chance was to make it back to the pier.

The two police officers walked through the door and opened the jail to let the culprits in. It was dark and musty. It smelled like a mixture of tobacco, beer, and very high humidity. There were no windows, just candles. Andrea looked at Eric with hunger in her eyes and longed for his touch. Andrea looked at Eric one last time.

"Okay, you're coming with me. The women's wing is around the corner."

The police officer pushed Andrea through the door frame. Andrea's shoulder bumped into the side.

"Ow, you pushed me into the door."

"Shut up, witch." He grabbed a night stick and whacked her thigh. She screamed out and fell to the floor. Eric heard her scream.

"Hey, what the hell are you guys doing to her? You touch one hair on her head, and I swear you're going to piss blood in the morning!" Eric yelled.

The two cops looked at each other and laughed. One grabbed Eric's shoulders and slammed his knee into Eric's abdomen. Eric let out a gasp as all the wind was knocked out of him. The other cop snickered and backhanded him across the face. Tears of anger rolled down Eric's face. All he could do was wheeze. No air went into his lungs, and Eric started to hyperventilate. The cops shrugged and threw Eric to the floor of the open cell.

Eric cried in the middle of the cell and curled up into a ball. Soft whimpers came out. While he sniffled, his breath started to come back. He picked himself up. He was locked away with a drunken bastard asleep on a bench. The man was scruffy and had a huge belly and a horrible haircut. Drool fell down his double chin. The man emitted a stench Eric had never smelled before. Eric looked down and saw that the man had pissed himself. Eric could have sworn he saw a fly walk into the man's mouth. Eric sat down on the other bench.

Andrea was aggressively handled, and she could have sworn the cop tried to feel her up when he guided her to the cell.

The other cop opened the cell, and they threw her in. He kept the door open.

"Hey Jacob, stand by the door. This one is a pretty lady."

The cop walked into the cell.

"Aren't you going to undo the restraints?" Andrea demanded.

The cop chuckled, "Not until I am done with you."

His smile grew eerie and the whites disappeared from his eyes. He started to crawl over her. Andrea let out an agonizing cry for help. A woman behind Andrea rushed over and rammed her shoulder into the officer. The officer was stunned. He lost his balance and rolled backwards. She gave him a couple kicks to push him past the cell door, which she shut right away.

"Get out of here, you wicked pig of a man!" the woman screamed out.

"Hey George, knock it off. The chief is coming," Jacob said. George stood up and looked Andrea square in the eyes. "Burn in hell, cunt. I hope the rope strangles you to death. And you'll wish the rope will take you out of your misery." He spat on her dress and walked away.

"Thank you so much, miss. I am so grateful for your help," Andrea pleaded.

"Don't mention it, darling."

Andrea looked at the woman. Her face was bruised and cut. Her dress had tears and splats of blood towards the bottom.

"Don't worry, this was from before I got to jail," she explained. "My husband and I were bickering. It escalated into a quarrel. I don't have to worry about him anymore. He was taken care of." She looked at Andrea and raised an eyebrow. "I swear to you these cages were not built to keep prisoners in, but to keep us protected from those wretched men."

Andrea was satisfied with the information she received and sat on the bench.

...

"Hey."

Eric turned swiftly. He didn't see the other person sitting down, but another individual was in the corner.

"You look like a straight-up fellow. Why are you here?"

Eric paused. He was conflicted about answering.

"They accused me of witchcraft."

"Huh, I thought all that stuff was nonsense. I thought the government was rounding up citizens who kept causing trouble. Being declared a witch is the kiss of death. No trial, just execution. Hung like a fucking dog. What's even worse is the people love it. They gather round to watch the execution of a proclaimed evil. I tell you, it's a scam to shush any coup to overthrow the King. It's a goddamn license to murder." The inmate spat at the ground when he said it.

"Interesting. Have you seen witches around here?" Eric asked.

"Eh, not one. The cops are lying bastards. I heard about this one guy at the pub. Turns out he was just using strings to fool people at Three-card Monte. He was no witch bearing magic, just your average crook," the man went on.

"Well, I have to ask, why are you in here?" Eric asked.

The man scoffed.

"You shouldn't really be asking that. But if you must insist, I robbed a shoe store not too far from here. I used to work there, but got fired because times were tough for the store. I get it, but that just makes my situation worse. If the whole country is suffering, why put the workforce on the street? We make this town run. So, I figured I had an in, since I knew where everything was kept. I ran in mud. It dried overnight. Because the cobbler makes one-of-a-kind heels, the detective here, Finn · top-notch chap · knew exactly who the footprints belonged to. The inspector found them and the owner pointed the finger at me. Enough about me; can you really do magic?"

"It's a long story."

The inmate scanned the room, knocked on the steel bars, and looked back at Eric. "Seems we have some time."

Eric started talking about how he had received the powers. He was finishing up explaining, "Now I just imagine things and somehow they appear in my hand. Kinda like magic," Eric explained.

The man stared at Eric and scanned him from head to toe. "So, you're telling me you can conjure up anything your mind wants, All because of a drink you and your lover made?"

"Yes."

"I've heard worse stories at the pub."

"What's your name?" Eric asked. The man shot daggers out of his eyes towards Eric. He stood up and approached until he was an inch away from Eric's face. "I don't have a name. But you may call me Leo. I need a favor from you. I have been in these drawers for quite some time. Over the past couple of days, they have gotten damp. I'm developing a rash of sorts. Could you give me a new pair, lad?"

Eric agreed. He reached into his pocket and pulled out nothing, but Leo saw what he needed to see. Leo reached out for the pair of drawers and stashed them away. "My god, you weren't lying. How long have you lived a life of crime?" the man questioned.

"To be honest, not long. I never do anything bad," Eric replied.

"Yes, that is apparent. I have a proposition. An eye for an eye makes the world go blind. Aye, a favor for a favor makes the world stay rich. You have the ability to get us out of here. There is a time where all guards go to sleep in their homes. I want you to fancy up some sort of key. And I can help you in return."

Eric sat and thought about it. He wondered what would happen if they escaped. His best plan was to head to the docks and sail away into the night.

"Okay, you have yourself a deal."

Leo nodded.

The two prisoners waited until the last guard left his post. Eric made different keys for Leo to try.

"The time has come, chap. Work your magic."

Eric rushed over to the door to try all the keys he made, but they kept failing. He felt defeated.

Leo got impatient and told Eric, "Hand over two metal sticks, thin."

Eric crafted the two sticks and handed them over. Within seconds they heard a click, and the door started to creak slowly open. Leo pushed through it and walked towards the entrance.

"Hey, I thought you were going to help me?" Eric cried out.

"Hm, see, you failed on your part; I took over. Also, let me give you a tip: never trust a crook." Leo slipped away into the night.

Eric was frustrated, but he realized his mistake. He rushed over to Andrea's cell and started working on the lock. The noise of metal clanging woke Andrea up. She saw Eric trying to free her and ran over to touch his face.

"There's no way in hell I will leave you. Just give me a minute," Eric said. He tried all his keys, but gave up. He tried the new trick his cellmate had taught him.

He formed two metal sticks and stuck them in the keyhole. After several minutes, the lock made a click sound. Andrea's eyes burst with joy. Eric opened the gate and grabbed her hand.

"Just wait." She ran over to the lady who helped her earlier and tapped her shoulder. Andrea waved to the lady to come out. The woman checked to see if the coast was clear and waltzed out with the couple.

Eric and Andrea made a mad dash towards the pier. They found their parking spot and jumped onto the boat. They undocked and took to the seas. They hugged and didn't let go. The water was calm, but the wind was sharp and cold. Above them was a malicious cloud that started to approach. But the couple was clueless, lost in each other's company. The boat started to rock.

Waves were pulling them in every direction when a bolt of lightning flashed across the sky, followed by a raging clap of thunder.

"Shit, looks like we floated into a storm. I hope our boat can take it."

The moon was overhead, and it shone onto the ship. The boat took a beating. It was thrown any way the sea wanted. Water started to fill the ship. Andrea and Eric grew worried. The boat was steady, but its direction was off. They felt like the boat was climbing. Eric looked over and noticed the boat was on top of a hundred-foot crest that was ready to smash it to pieces.

"Here, put this on. It's a life vest," Eric shouted, handing one over to Andrea. "The boat is not going to be able to sustain this fall. Here's a flare so we can find each other if we get split up.".

Andrea trembled and tears rolled down her cheeks. But she had no other choice but to accept her fate. The boat arrived at the top of the wave, and what felt like an eternity only spanned seconds. The boat went free-falling towards the ocean at a tremendous velocity. The couple braced for impact as the boat smashed into the water and crumbled to pieces. Both Andrea and Eric were knocked unconscious from the impact.

Eric and Andrea lay motionless, wet, and out cold. Each floated on a piece of debris. The storm had passed, but the wind and current were strong. With every passing second, the couple grew farther apart. The storm had won. Two loving hearts were broken to shambles by the mighty power of the ocean. The darkness crept along for hours before the sun rose. The couple drifted, separated by the vast ocean, floating farther into the wet abyss.

CHAPTER 5: F.E.A.R.

The couple floated across the ocean, the waves guiding their direction. Eric drifted in and out of consciousness. He rubbed his eyes. Finally, he was able to open them, and he stared deep into the big blue sky. The sun shot rays down into his corneas.

"Ugh, what the hell? It feels like I've been hit by a Mack Truck. Hey Andrea, how are you doing?"

He waited, but the pause was too long. Eric sat up, worried. He looked to see what was left of their boat. His eyes widened and he noticed he was floating on a chunk of wood.

"ANDREA! ANDREA!" Eric yelled as loudly as he could, but his voice disappeared into the vast ocean. A part of him was missing.

The floating piece of wood was no bigger than a queen-sized mattress. He looked in the distance and noticed a small piece of land emerging on the horizon. Eric saw a piece of broken wood next to him, so he picked it up and started paddling towards land.

Andrea laid motionless on the floating platform. The sun beat down, pinning her to the piece of wood. Andrea struggled to get up. All her energy was sapped away. Her platform floated onto a sandy little island. She started to wake up from the sound of seagulls squawking all around her. Dazed and confused, she sat up, and only saw a tiny beach.

"Where the hell are we?"

Andrea stood up when no one answered but the wind. Andrea panicked. She had lost Eric. She drew her hand to her mouth and started biting her nails. Desperate to find him, she started searching the small island. It was no bigger than a football field, but it was densely packed with vegetation in the middle. All of the trees blocked her view of what was on the other side. An eerie silence was heard. Once the seagulls stopped making noise, a low hissing sound filled her ears.

The dense forest was getting closer. Words started to form in the sand. They read, *Love and paradise just up ahead.* Bewildered, Andrea smiled at the thought. A sign pointed in a certain direction. She was accustomed to the arcane environment and blindly followed.

Eric frantically searched for Andrea, but he started to lose hope when he noticed how small the island was. The sun shone brightly on him, so he took cover in the shade provided by the trees. He dragged his feet in the sand. When he looked down, he noticed words that read, *Love and paradise just up ahead.*

He looked until the wind blew away the words. Reading them put him in a cheery mood. He looked up ahead and saw an arrow pointing towards the jungle. That was his best chance. The couple blazed through the jungle separately. Each one got closer to their partner the deeper they went into the jungle.

They each saw a cliff with no visible bottom. A ten-foot gap opened between the two cliffs. The couple soon recognized each other from across the way. They were relieved about how close they were.Before either of them could say a word, the ground shook violently, and the gap between the couple started to stretch.

"Eric!"

"Andrea!"

Each yelled out their partner's name. But it was no use; within seconds, they were out of sight.

Eric stood next to a natural rock wall. His mind tried to comprehend what had just happened. His mind was rattled and his heart was empty. He saw the floor crumble away beneath him. All he could feel was defeat. He tucked his head in between his legs. Eric let out the deepest sigh of his life. His chest felt like it had ripped in half, and his stomach ached in pain. A blue shadow emerged from his body. Eric stayed huddled against the wall. He felt empty of motivation to continue.

Eric put his hands over his eyes, holding back whimpers. She was so close; he saw her figure. It felt like someone put a 20-pound iron sphere in his stomach. His heart was in his throat. Eric walked over to the edge of the cliff and sat in silence before he attempted to move.

He tried to gather his thoughts, but they ran away like loose chickens. Eric picked himself up and started to walk along the wall. He noticed a brass doorknob on the wall. Eric shrugged his shoulders and figured that was the way out.

When he opened the door, he found himself in a hallway. The hallway was very dim. Eric could barely see the ceiling. When he looked down the hall, the end disappeared into a gentle, fading glow. The carpet was decorated with a maroon, blue, and gold paisley pattern. The wallpaper was floral with a deep crimson background. Eric was a little confused; he saw no doors that led anywhere else. There was usually a sign that displayed which direction to take, but not this time. The hallway looked like it stretched far.

He randomly picked a direction. His walk was slow and cautious. The low lighting made Eric anxious. The floorboards creaked and the lights flickered. There was a strange, high-pitched whirring sound. It all fed into Eric's brain. He thought of limitless outcomes.

"What if something comes from behind? What if something grabs me? What if something is looking at me? This place looks abandoned. No one is here, but it's an operational facility."

A door started to approach in Eric's vision. The door's plaque read, *Caution: Fear Ahead*. It made Eric very uneasy, but he knew that it was going to be his only choice.

Eric stepped through the door. Out in the distance he saw three shadowy figures. Eric turned back to look at the door, but it shrank into its center. The door disappeared.

The room had a creepy industrial vibe to it. Everything was concrete. It looked like a jail with no windows and no color: just a dull stone wall. The place had a cold chill near the walls. The environment made Eric grow unsettled.

A sound scurried behind Eric. *Pa pa pa pa.* He turned his head quickly to see what had joined him in the room. He scanned the room with a keen eye, but nothing moved. Paranoia crept into Eric's psyche, making him feel on edge and jumpy. Eric walked up to a wall and touched it. It had three green circles inscribed on the concrete. Eric was puzzled.

He found a potential exit: a very large boulder blocked an entryway, and there was light shining through the cracks. Eric turned and saw hallways that branched out from the room he was in. There were three rooms at the ends of the hallways, like prongs on a trident. Eric began to explore the labyrinth.

Eric made the decision to go to the hallway on the right. His mom always told him to tie his shoes starting with the right one because the left side was evil.

He started to get used to his surroundings, which reminded him of a factory. At the end of the hallway was a room. He walked in and discovered it was a small room. In the center of the room was a concrete pillar with a floating, glowing green circle above it. Eric was mesmerized by the glow. Upon closer inspection, the circle was the same size as the circle on the wall in the first room. He grabbed it and went back into the main room and approached the wall. He held the ring up against the wall. The ring lifted out of his hands and floated into the left circle.

He figured the other rings must be in the middle hallway and the left hallway. Behind Eric were the same four sounds. Eric stayed vigilant. Something was making the noise. Eric chose the middle hallway next. It had a similar room at the end. There was another green circle, and he took it back. He held it up and it floated to the right-side spot. The middle circle was empty. Eric walked towards the left hallway. The noises came back, but with greater intensity. It was close. Eric jumped as he saw three shadowy figures get closer. Their definition was starting to show. Three dogs appeared, but they were like no dogs he had ever seen before. Each hound was stripped of its skin, showing only muscle and tendons with blood saturating the delicate muscular system. Drops of crimson hit the floor, leaving a trail of blood where they walked.

Eric's eyes widened with fear. Memories of his uncle's dog biting his arm when he was 13 years old flooded his mind. His uncle had invited him over for lunch one Saturday. His uncle had shown him his Rottweiler named Bruce. Eric was impressed with the size and the coat of the dog. He approached Eric. He squatted to pet the fluffy being. Eric combed its hair on the top, patted him and gave him a good rub. The dog did not seem to mind. The dog started sniffing Eric's arm as he went to scratch the canine's neck. A loud sound cracked: two cars T-boned on the street. The dog was startled. Bruce snarled and wrinkled his snout, opened his jaws, and clamped onto Eric's arm.

Eric did not have time to react. Eric was fast, but the dog was faster. Bruce pierced his canines into his arm. Eric felt powerless; the dog had complete control. Eric screamed bloody murder while the Rottweiler growled deeply. Eric could feel the clamping force in the bite; Eric felt like his bone was getting crushed. His flashback ended and he needed somewhere to take cover.

There was a wall to hide behind. He peeked around the corner. The pack was walking and sniffing objects. The greyhounds were missing their eyes. In their eye sockets were black holes where death lived comfortably. Eric trembled in terror.

The dogs were close by and Eric feared they could hear him breathing. He slowly creeped to the other corner, undetected. The hounds stood in the path of the last room, where he could see the glowing circle. There was no way he could get by them; the hallway was too narrow.

Eric thought he could hide in a corner. His shoelace was untied, and he tripped on it. His feet shuffled, and he regained his balance. When he looked up, the dogs were staring directly at him.

Eric ran.

He sprinted down the hallway, whimpering in fear. Their shuffling paws were getting closer to him. One snarled loudly. Eric knew it was too close. Outrunning them seemed impossible. As he approached a corner, he banked around it, hard. His right foot slipped under him. Eric stumbled forward. He picked up speed again until he felt a pinch. The pinch came from his leg. A dog had clamped on his heel.

"Oh, shit."

His adrenaline was at an all-time high. Slamming to the floor, he covered his head as the other dogs arrived.

He waited with his eyes closed. Opening them, he saw the room he had started in. Eric looked up at the three inscribed circles. The green rings were gone!

"Whoa. I'm gonna need to sit down for this one."

His stomach felt heavy and his body tingled. He felt sensitive, like a victim of a brutal mauling of canines.

Eric started to compose himself.

"The rings floated in certain directions. They didn't float towards the spots I held them to. There are only three hallways and three rings. Hm, I wish I had Andrea right now," he groaned loudly. The sound of a pitter patter from paws came back. The sound got louder, and he could see the dogs appear in the distance.

"Oh, you gotta be kidding me!"

The dogs ran towards Eric as he closed his eyes and braced for impact.

He opened his eyes and found himself in the same room again. He was on the floor and his body ached like it would have the day after a heavy workout.

Huh, I guess I should stay quiet, he thought. *I need to figure out how to avoid the dogs. They can't see, but they can hear pretty damn well. If I know where the dogs are, I can avoid them. The first time I went right, middle, and left. I should check the middle one.*

Eric creeped over to the middle hallway and looked into the room. The dogs were patrolling. When he went to the left hallway, there was nothing. The ring was waiting to be taken, so he grabbed the ring from the left room and held it up to its spot on the concrete wall. The first ring floated left and the second ring floated right.

He went to the right room and took the ring. After grabbing the ring, he went back to the concrete wall and raised it to the carving.

Eric felt confident. He had added two of the three rings to the carvings. To complete the pattern, he just needed one more ring. The middle room was vacant, and there was no sign of the dogs anywhere. He grabbed the last ring and ran back to the main room as quickly as possible. Eric held the ring up, and it hovered towards the middle carving.

The green rings floated up into the air. They glowed with a radioactive hue. All three rings came together and formed one massive ring. The ring turned around and faced the boulder. It shot towards the massive rock and blew it into a thousand pieces of glitter. Eric was astonished

The boulder started to shift right. It slid all the way across the floor. Eric saw a little glowing pink heart above the entrance. He smiled and walked in.

...

Andrea was alone in the forest. Andrea was elated to see Eric, but her feelings were shattered when the ground tore apart. She paused and decided to take long, deep breaths to calm herself down. *In and out. Repeat.*

Good comes in, bad goes out, she thought. She started walking to get her mind away from being pessimistic.

Her brisk walk led her to a trail with a small house. It looked cute. She called out to see if anyone was around. No one responded. She went up to the door, knocked, and waited. Andrea figured no one was home and turned the knob. It opened to her delight.

"I have been used to every door being locked until this one. Just like the real world. All these closed doors."

She entered the home. The home was small and cute. Books were everywhere and little picture frames covered every surface of the wall. There was no spot unfilled with a trinket. The house had plenty of life. But there was another door. Andrea knew that was the way out. Above the door was a sign that said, *Watch your step.* Andrea thought about it for a while and walked through. The door took her outside, next to the face of a cliff. There were tons of cactuses around.

"Shit, not this again."

Andrea walked close to the edge. Her hands started to sweat and her knees began to tremble at the height of the fall.

"Goddamn, I hate heights."

Andrea looked down the cliff and could barely see the ground. She walked along the edge and noticed a button sticking out of a rock. It looked normal to her.

"I might as well try it." She pressed the button and the ground shook. Off in the distance, a fast-moving object headed towards Andrea. She was hesitant, but backed away from the edge. A floating rock came close to the edge. She walked closer to the platform. It was several feet away from where she was standing.

"There's no bridge? Why couldn't this be easy? Oh god, I really hope I don't have to jump across."

Andrea was exhausting her options. The cliff edge was more desert than the woodlands. A tree could be fashioned into a bridge, she reasoned, but there was nothing long enough. She figured she was going to have to jump, whether she liked it or not.

"Ugh, this just had to be it, huh. Heights. Who made this place? I hate you!"

Andrea did quick breathing exercises to help her calm down before she jumped. She was terrified. One small misstep and she would plunge down to her doom.

"Okay, relax. There could be a hint that could help me," Andrea said to herself.

She looked around the cliff edge and found nothing. Her stomach got heavier. Andrea looked directly at the platform. One foot went in front of the other and she leaned forward. A running start would be the only way she could make it across. Running closer to the edge, she lept off her back foot and directly onto the platform.

Her landing made her lose balance, but she was able to stick it. Andrea let out a small, high-pitched cry of joy. The next platform hovered over to her. She was able to maneuver across each platform that came her way. Her confidence grew, and her fear of heights receded. The next platform was an oddly-shaped rock. It was small on one side and big on the other; a very oblong shape. Andrea took time to look at it and think about how she should jump and land.

She jumped across and cleared one edge, but the tip of her foot got caught under the rock. Her stomach hit the rock first and she slid across. The rock was smooth; there were no protrusions to grab onto. She overcalculated the jump and slid off the rock.

Falling took forever. Her back faced the ground and her head faced the sky. Andrea wept in her last seconds. Andrea thought of all the things she had and hadn't done. Smack! She hit the ground.

Suddenly, Andrea revived. She gasped for air; all of it had been knocked out of her system. Her eyes were wide, and she tried to open her mouth to breathe again. More tears came. She had no idea what to say or how to comprehend what had happened. Everything flashed before her eyes, including her family, friends, father, and mother. Her imagination showed a funeral with her entire family in attendance. She realized one of the toughest pains of being a parent is losing a child.

Andrea needed to catch her breath. She felt delusional.

"Did I just *die*? Oh my god, that was the worst experience ever! I only had seconds left to live. Everything and nothing mattered. My poor parents · I could never let them go through that."

The desolate landscape didn't help her situation. There was no one to confide in, no one to help her. Anxiety creeped into her mind, but she had to continue.

Andrea stood up from the ground and saw she had been dropped right where she started. After she looked at the rocks, she brushed herself off and thought about her jumps from the previous attempt.

Andrea was fixing her clothing when she heard shuffling behind her. Her neck whipped around and she saw a person standing right behind her.

"Who are you?"

"I'm with postal. You have mail." The mailman leaned over and gave Andrea a letter. Andrea was hesitant, but ended up taking the letter. The mailman nodded and walked into the distance. Andrea opened the letter: it was a letter from her parents. Her eyes welled with tears. She couldn't contain her emotions as she realized how much they meant to her. At the bottom it was signed, *Love, Mom and Dad.* Andrea's attitude changed as she read the letter. Her confidence came back, and the fear of death disappeared.

A feeling of guilt passed through. She slightly enjoyed the rush of being near death, but she shook off that thought. Andrea looked directly at the platform and took her jump. The rock was far, but she leapt into the air and nailed the landing.

Nothing was going to stop her now. She reached the odd-shaped stone from before. Andrea overcame her fear and she jumped with all her might. The rock swayed side to side, but she didn't lose her footing. Andrea looked ahead and saw another piece of land. She smiled. All she had to do was keep jumping towards the next platform. She jumped with all of her might and finally reached the end. Andrea stood on solid ground.

"Hell yeah! Take that, you cursed place. I can't believe the gall this place has to torture people like this."

The desert landscape had a giant sand dune with an entrance. She walked closer to the hill and saw a cave with a glowing pink heart above it. Andrea realized this was the entrance and she walked in.

CHAPTER 6: HOPE YOU STUDIED

There was a big, beautiful white room. Pink accents complimented the sharp lines, and red was shown vibrantly. It resembled a lobby furnished with pink heart chairs in rows and columns. There were two separate hallways with pink and white LED lights along the ceiling. Eric and Andrea stood in the hallways. They were unaware of each other's presence. They both walked towards the middle. Eric saw something flash, and he felt scared. There was a corner to hide behind.

He peered over only to notice his lover. His eyes grew hungry, and the longing for her touch drove him wild. He ran out from the wall.

"*Andrea!*" Eric ran towards her. She was startled at first, and squinted her eyes to adjust to the new light. Eric's shape started to fill in her vision. She jumped up and ran towards him. They met with an embrace. Their bodies met and they felt each other's warmth.

"I have missed you so much! I thought I was going to get out without seeing you. The last maze was really fucked up," Andrea said, and her breath turned into a whimper.

"Holy shit, I can't believe what I had to go through. I don't even want to know what you had to go through." They hugged in silence.

"I love you," Andrea whispered.

"I love you, too."

The couple couldn't let go of each other; it was love at its purest. They were two different people with great chemistry. They came from different backgrounds, but found common interests. More importantly, they cared for each other. It was a bond that could rival the love of a parent.

"This place looks like a relief. I can't believe what happened," Andrea said.

"Tell me about it. I felt like the machine was looking into my mind. Like, the dogs - seriously? The one thing I'm terrified of. At least I feel cozy in this little waiting room," Eric said.

"Wow, I get what you are saying. Honestly, fucking heights? That is my worst fear. There is no way that it's random for everybody. This place is wacky. We started floating around in the air! Imagine they made a custom maze for every group? That's impossible," Andrea replied.

"Yeah, I get what you are saying. It has to be a complicated feedback system. I haven't seen any cameras, though. Somehow, the machine must be watching us," Eric said.

Andrea and Eric stood in silence, thinking. The couple enjoyed each other's company. Without saying anything, they felt each other's thoughts. The couple was comfortable with their silence, which was a true mark of the strength of the relationship. The couple searched the room.

The room was brighter than all the rooms they had explored. The white and pink hues made the walls pop. It was a perfect opportunity for the couple to take a rest and regain their energy. They plopped on the chairs and both let out a sigh. Eric closed his eyes and tilted his head back. He got lost in his mind. Andrea stretched across the chair and felt the extension of her muscles. They both knew they would have to continue the perilous maze. "Can we get ice cream after this?" Andrea asked.

"Of course. And a nice big meal."

The couple started fantasizing about eating a hot dinner and ice cream for dessert. They each got lost in a daydream, but shook out of it.

"We need to find a new exit. I know it's been a long ride so far. There's no one else I would rather do this maze with," Eric told Andrea, and she blushed.

"Look at you, being all sentimental. You would not believe how much I missed and needed you. I felt a pain in my heart when we got separated, and I could not live with that. You mean everything to me," Andrea said.

Eric saw love in Andrea's eyes. Sincerity and passion filled her pupils while she looked at Eric.

"I felt completely defeated. I was losing the will to go on without you. I was so scared. Everything loses value when the thought of losing you comes to mind. But when we are together, we can defeat anything," said Eric.

Auras of compassion hovered over the couple. Their frequencies synced together and created a perfect harmony of signals. A spark flickered between the two. They kept holding tight and didn't ever want to let go.

Their hug loosened, but their love strengthened.

"I think we should start looking for a way out of here," Eric said.

"I agree. Look at how far we have come!" Andrea added.

A neon sign appeared on the wall. It read, *Just a hop, skip, and jump away.* Eric called Andrea over.

"I guess we're getting closer to the end?" Andrea exclaimed.

"Yeah I think so. We have gotten through a lot of rooms. I'm sure it's not too far away."

They were both confident about moving forward. They started to walk side by side. Andrea leaned closer to Eric as they walked. Her hand brushed up against his. First their pinkies grabbed a hold of each other, and then they held hands. Their connection was firm and strong, and they felt invincible. The couple found another arrow. The right path was shown to them. Their bodies tingled with feel-good chemicals as they rushed into their brains. A wave of pleasure and release flowed through them.

They reached the end of the hallway, and a door started to faze in. Eric rubbed his eyes because the door seemed out of focus. He looked confused and shook his head to make sure nothing was wrong with his eyesight.

Eric turned to Andrea and said,"Are you seeing this too? Like, the door is all fuzzy. It seems out of focus."

"I definitely see it. It's weird, but there's no lock on it. Which is surprisingly stranger for this place than the blurry door. You should try to open it," Andrea said.

Eric nodded in agreement. He walked closer to the door, and it opened. The couple was surprised.

"That was a little too easy," Eric said.

Andrea laughed. "No way that was it. Let's go through the door first, Mr. Optimistic."

Eric chuckled. When they walked in, the couple was taken aback. The whole room looked like a game show stage. Eric and Andrea were both in awe. The room had everything, from lighting and cabling to a stage and video cameras. The room was black and had blue LEDs in the ceiling along the edges. Two podiums were in the middle of the stage. In the center of each podium was Eric and Andrea's names, respectively.

They both laughed and had a smile on their face. Each went to their own podium. A letter sat on each podium, waiting for them. They looked at each other and figured they should open them. The same message appeared on both letters. They read:

Welcome, and thank you for traveling this far. You are close to the finish line, but not yet done. You will enter our gameshow. Both partners must answer until a combined score of 3000 is met. Every question answered correctly will earn 500 points. However, a penalty will be given for every wrong answer. Have fun and enjoy the rest of the maze.

The couple was excited to play. A giant screen turned on in front of them. Giant letters appeared that read, *Ready?* The couple looked at each other and yelled "Yes!" in unison.

The screen fizzled to a low, glowing black. The stage went silent and the lights dimmed. Darkness enveloped the room for a moment. Two spotlights pointed at the podiums. Eric and Andrea were the center of attention. The screen started to flash, along with the stage lighting. Eric's name appeared on the screen.

"Okay, I guess it's supposed to be my turn. Can you help me, Andrea?" He looked over his shoulder and noticed something was wrong. Andrea touched the spot where her mouth was supposed to be. She looked directly at him, and he noticed something horrible had happened:

Andrea's mouth had disappeared from her face. A fear inside of her started to grow.

Eric took a big gulp and looked at the screen, which displayed a question: *What guided you across the rose garden?*

The answer immediately came to Eric's mind. "The smell of the roses!" he shouted.

The screen faded away. Eric waited a little while. Suddenly, the screen read, *Correct!*

Eric cheered in excitement. But the sound of his cheer changed. He kept yelling, but his voice got quieter. His mouth squeezed slowly inwards until his lips disappeared from his face. He put his hands on his face, but felt nothing.

"Ah!" Andrea shouted. "Oh wait, I can talk again! This is great. Hey Eric! Oh… ha! That's what happened to me! Sucker. It's not that bad once you realize you can breathe through your nose."

Andrea turned her head to the screen.

What shape is the building?

Andrea stood quietly and thought about the question before she shouted an answer. She was very patient; she didn't want to rush into any wrong answers. Andrea thought to herself, *Who knows what penalties they will give us if we get it wrong? Oh my gosh, I really hope I don't get this wrong, I would hate it if we got hurt. What if they send out bees? That would hurt so much. What if they target just one of us for the penalty? I can't handle this, I need to breathe.*

Andrea took a couple of breaths and looked at Eric. He had no mouth, but he smiled with his eyes. Andrea took the time to think about her answer. The building was next to a corporate center, next to an apartment. Just a random box building. Really square. Perfectly square.

"The building is a cube!"

The screen glowed black, waiting to give a response. Andrea was timid until it read out, *Correct!*

"Whew, that was close! I was just about to..." but Andrea's mouth completely vanished.

"Guess it's my turn again. Show me what you got," Eric said.

The screen fizzled with reds and blues. White letters flowed to the screen. *What gave you away at the English harbor?-*

Eric was struck with guilt. His face blushed. The machine watched the whole time. Eric had to think hard. He remembered being at the pub.

"Something happened with a stranger. The cops arrived immediately and escorted Andrea and me away for selling an imaginary pocket watch."

Andrea nodded. The screen went blank before it read, *Correct!* Eric had disappointment in his eyes. It had clearly been his mistake. He felt shame for his selfish actions. He didn't say a peep before his mouth vanished. Andrea looked at him deeply. Before she could say anything, the screen took her attention. On a green screen, brown words came up.

Currently at 1500 points. Halfway to match point. Andrea, what color was the rabbit that led you away from the shadow people?

Memories of the creatures came back. A sudden chill ran up her spine. The way they had come off the wall and moved towards the couple was too lifelike. They had no regard for the safety of the couple. Despite her fear, Andrea dug deep in her memories. The little bunny started to appear in her mind. The bunny ran into the lake and they followed it. Andrea closed her eyes and thought hard. She remembered the cute little fella. He had caught her eye in the rose gardens.

"The bunny was white!" Andrea yelled at the screen. The machine stayed silent while it processed her answer.

Correct!

Andrea was relieved that she was correct.

Eric cheered when his mouth appeared. He waited for his question on the screen. A red background showed up with blue letters on the screen.

What was the name of the inmate that you helped to escape?

Andrea was confused; she didn't remember another person. Eric must have run into another person. It wasn't completely impossible, as she had run into another woman.

Eric was stumped. He was good at faces, but bad with names. "Um, ugh. Dammit, why can't I remember that guy's name? We talked for a while, but he was reluctant to give me his name. What if he gave me the wrong name? Oh boy, this is gonna be bad. Pat!" The machine took time to think about Eric's answer.

The couple waited for the machine's reply. *Incorrect.*

Eric was morose. He heard sirens and flashing red alarms on the ceiling above. A clear plastic tube fell from the ceiling and onto Eric. He was stuck in the tight confinement of the tube. Andrea tried to scream for help, but her mouth remained lost. Andrea looked towards the top of the tube and noticed pink mist falling onto Eric. Andrea pointed towards the top for Eric to see.

A mist fell directly on him. He was terrified of whatever crazy effect the mist would have on him. The mist started clouding his vision. A tingly sensation filled Eric's nose. It ventured up his nostrils, and a rush of air filled his lungs. Eric let out a sneeze and couldn't stop sneezing.

Andrea was confused. Her mouth started to reappear.

"Eric, what's happening?" she yelled out, but it was too late. Eric's mouth had already vanished.

The pink mist did not stop. Eric's body had no way of sneezing. Stuck in the loop between sneezing and not sneezing. He became incapable of letting it all out. The sneezes backfired into his chest and never left his body. The satisfaction of letting out a big *ah-choo* was mercilessly ripped away from Eric.

The screen asked Andrea the next question. Purple and gold lettering appeared that read, *What item let you float?*

Andrea thought, but she thought slowly. Her boyfriend suffered more and more the longer she took. She glanced over at Eric and saw his eyes filling up with tears. The backed-up sneezes made his tear glands swell up. Eric cried and suffered from constriction.

Andrea thought about her answer carefully. She knew it was right before they made it to the English dock. They had been in a room, looking at a painting that let them merge into a new world. Andrea thought harder.

Visions of a counter started to come back. She thought about floating.

"Root beer float!" Andrea told the machine. The machine paused and thought about the answer. The machine took an eternity before replying. Andrea waited in anticipation.

Correct! it read. More green and blue lights flashed in their faces.

The tube lifted away from Eric. Andrea's mouth disappeared right after she blew him a kiss. It was a fading kiss, her lips will disappear in a few seconds.

Eric's mouth started to reappear. "*Ah-choo!* Oh, my lord. Thank you so much. You have no idea how relieving that was. Man, I really hope we get this question right so we can get the hell outta here. This one is for you, baby!"

Eric pointed his finger towards his lover. The creases in her eyes gave the illusion of a smile. Eric faced the omnipotent machine. The white screen faded into a gradient orange. Words showed up on the screen.

What did Andrea's fear room contain?

Andrea's eyes grew to the size of platters. All she got from Eric was a look of confusion. His confidence was completely sucked out of him.

Andrea knew the answer. *If only Eric had listened to me, we could actually win this thing. Thank god if he gets it wrong, something bad happens to him and not me. Let's hear what he has to say. Maybe he will get lucky,"* Andrea thought.

Eric was timid, and he did not answer quickly. He looked at Andrea, but she had nothing to say. Eric was worried. His nerves built up, and anxiety creeped in.

"Snakes!" he blurted out.

Andera gave him a quizzical look. *I can't believe he got it wrong. That fool! Why do I even bother? He's lucky he's cute,* she thought to herself.

Eric sulked. The machine had not yet responded with the answer, but the look on Andrea's face told him everything.

"Okay, bring it on!" Eric shouted before his mouth started to vanish.

Incorrect! The machine showed Eric. Sirens and flashing lights went off. The tube swallowed Eric again. Andrea looked at him helplessly. Eric put his hand on the tube.

A quick flash of light blinded Andrea, and she looked away. When she looked back at Eric, he was frozen. His body was enveloped in dark blue ice. His hand remained on the glass and his gaze stayed fixed upon her.

"No!" Andrea shouted. Her breathing became rapid. Her words fumbled out of her mouth as she tried to make sense of what had happened. She looked at Eric and tears flowed from her eyes. Andrea's heart felt heavy. The look on his face was innocent, and his eyes betrayed fear. Andrea began to weep. The machine paused. It knew the contestant was going through emotional turmoil. It did not rush the contestant. The machine waited.

Andrea sniffled. She stopped to look at the machine for a second. The screen was blank. It displayed a soft white glow that faded into pale blue.

"Why did the machine wait for me?" she thought aloud. She noticed the screen took a little longer for the words to appear. "That's strange. It's lagging a little bit. Hm, when I started getting ready, the screen changed colors. It's waiting for me... This must be the machine that's controlling all of the rooms!"

A little green light lit up the screen. Andrea saw the flash.

"Ha, I knew it. Whoa, I can't wait to tell Eric. Alright machine, I'm ready." Pixels on the screen made a wave, like a virtual nod of agreement.

What was Eric's fear room?

The machine waited for Andrea's reply.

"Dogs!"

Moments went by in utter silence. Andrea waited in anticipation.

Correct!

"Yes! Just one more question and we're one step closer to the end."

When she finished talking, her mouth shrank and fell off her face. Andrea got goosebumps. She stared at Eric in the hopes he would become free. The tube fell into the ground, but the crystal structure remained. A tiny hammer mechanism opened from the ceiling. It gave the structure a sharp blow. The mechanism retracted back into the ceiling.

At first, nothing happened. But then a sharp crack resonated from somewhere in the crystal. A louder snap came, and a network of visible fractures ran across the ice. The structure could not take the inner stress, and it shattered into a billion pieces. Shards flew towards Andrea. She shielded herself and tried to see Eric in the chaos. Eric's hand drooped down to the podium. He caught himself.

"Whoa! What happened?" He looked at Andrea, but realized her mouth had already disappeared.

Huh, well, I'm free, he thought. *I guess she must have gotten the question right. I love her so much. She's carrying this team for sure. Would you look at that: our score is in the bottom right corner. Two thousand out of three thousand! I just need to win this one, and Andrea could take it home! I hope my losing streak is over. I don't think I can take whatever they will dish out next,*

The machine waited until he was done thinking The words appeared on the screen.

How much did you pay for one entrance ticket?

Eric paused. He put his hand on his chin and gave it a thought.

"For fuck's sake!" Eric barked out. Andrea heard him and her eyeballs nearly hit the ceiling. Her frustration showed without her mouth; her eyes pierced into him. Andrea sat quietly even without a mouth. Eric looked up, hoping for a spark of memory to click. "It definitely was more than twenty dollars. Goddamn. How the hell am I supposed to know this? Huh? Who remembers those kinds of things? Nerds! Okay, I am just gonna think about it for a second. Think. Did I give him cash? I'm pretty sure I paid with my card." Eric gave it more thought. The pressure eased away, and Andrea was less tense.

Eric wrapped his hands on the railing in front of him. His head shot up quickly and his body stood straight up. A memory struck him. He thought about the first time they got to the building. He made a payment. His pocket had a crumpled piece of paper inside. Eric reached into his back pocket and grabbed the paper. A shriek came from him. Andrea looked at Eric, and he showed her what he had found. Her eyes grew wide, and she knew he would answer the question correctly. The machine waited for Eric's response. Eric looked down at his hand and read the receipt from when he purchased the tickets.

"Thirteen seventy-five!" he yelled out. The machine waited. It was slow to respond. It kept Eric on the tips of his toes. Eric started to grow weary.

"Correct!"

Eric cheered into the air and shouted something before his mouth grew wings and flew away. Andrea's mouth started to reappear.

"Good job, sweetie!" Andrea told Eric. He gave her a thumbs up and looked at her effortlessly. When she was ready, Andrea faced the machine. She paused, waited, and said, "I'm ready."

The machine waited. It changed colors. It faded into a soft orange, like sherbet. Black letters appeared on the screen. *What made you go blind in the library room?* the machine questioned.

Andrea took a step back and leaned on the railing. She looked up to see if the answers were on the edge of her brain. She tried to recollect the memories. They had faded ever so slightly over time; the crisp, finer details seem to blur. Andrea sat back and relaxed. The cauldron reappeared in her mind. Her thoughts were fleeting.

"I remember we had to mix a bunch of stuff together. What was it? I can feel it at the tip of my tongue. Um, I shot up to the ceiling. I remember staring at animals. There were a bunch of them · oh my god, they were staring right at me! Oh yes, the deer! It was squishy, and as soon as I grabbed it, my vision got blurry. The doe's eye!"

The machine heard Andrea. The machine pulsed a little and it took time to think. It waited, and so did Andrea. The score was 2500 out of 3000. They needed one last point to win. Eric waited for the screen to change, but nothing happened. He looked at Andrea and gave her an enamored gaze. The machine stopped whirring. The room fell silent, and the screen went dead. The lights went dim. Darkness fell like a curtain.

Two backlights behind the screen came on. Very softly, the screen turned on and gave a soft, static black glow. The screen showed letters: *Congratulations, you may move on.*

Eric cheered out along with Andrea. "Wait, I have my mouth back! And you do too!" he yelled.

Eric leapt over the railing with one hand and swung his feet over. He ran over to Andrea's podium and looked up at her. Andrea licked her lips. They made eye contact and were entranced by each other. Eric ran his finger across her lips.

"They're real," Andrea said in a whispering voice. Eric smiled salaciously. He put his hand on her cheek and pulled her in closer for a kiss. Her lips were soft, like a warm marshmallow. Andrea loved when Eric pulled her in. It fulfilled what anybody could want: to be loved.

"You ready?" Eric asked.

Andrea looked up at him. "You bet your ass."

CHAPTER 7: THE MARINER

The couple fixed their clothing before they got off the stage. They jumped off the stage and walked towards an open door towards the back.

"That was pretty fun! You know, besides getting all those wrong," Eric said.

"Yeah, you gotta work on your memory. It's pretty shoddy. Like that old pickup truck you used to have. Sometimes it would want to turn on, sometimes it wouldn't. Gosh, that thing was temperamental," Andrea said.

"Hey, don't bring Lupita into this. She was a great car that had good bones and was on her last legs. It's hard to recover from a cracked engine block. Sometimes they never recover."

Andrea punched the side of his arm. The couple walked together through the doors. They led to a small gray room. There was a hole in the center of the room. They walked around the hole and looked inside. In the hole was crystal clear water. A fish swam by. A noise diverted their attention to the ceiling. A sign held by chains lowered. It read, *Dive in, but before you do: have a dill, get a gill. What we have sung, will give you a lung.*

They both read the sign and thought about it. The sign was pulled into the ceiling. Two pickles arrived from a panel on the wall.

"I think we're supposed to eat them." Eric guessed.

The clue clicked for the couple. Eat the pickles.

They both walked over to the pickled vegetables. The couple ate them at the same time. After the pickles went down their throats, they could feel their bodies changing. It felt like a worm was wriggling from their toes to their necks. Their necks started to grow itchy. The area near each of their clavicles started to vibrate. The vibrations formed gills. They put their hands on the vibrating spots. The couple felt their skin change texture.

"Whoa, check it out - you have gills!" Eric yelled.

"So do you!" Andrea replied.

"Do you think they work?" Eric asked.

"I'm sure they do," Andrea responded.

"Only one way to find out," Eric told Andrea. Eric started to undress down to his boxers. The hole was right in front of him. He dove in front of Andrea. She saw him go under and waited for him to come up. Time faded away and she started to get a bit worried, but she figured he could probably breathe underwater. A quick flash of flesh swam by in the hole. Eric waved for her to come on in. She thought about it; it did look refreshing. Andrea took off her clothes and dove underwater. The cool water hit her face and the weightlessness of the water carried her away. They looked at each other. When they spoke, bubbles and muffles came out. The couple had to rely on hand signals. The gills only allowed them to breathe underwater, not speak.

They explored their surroundings and saw amazing wildlife. Schools of fish swam by. The scales on the fish had a sheen that reflected light beautifully. The sun rays beamed into the water and reflected all the different purples and oranges in the corals. There were small fish with yellow, white, and black circle markings. There were huge fish that looked only in one direction. Pretty orange and blue fish swam amongst the coral.

The couple were swimming together when they noticed a dolphin. Andrea waved towards Eric and pointed towards the dolphin. His eyes grew wide and he nodded his head in agreement. The couple started to swim in that direction. The dolphin's figure came into perspective as they approached it. But something was off; the fins seemed too long for a dolphin.

Eric and Andrea stopped swimming and looked closer. The water blurred the outline of the creature. They couldn't get a clear image of what it was. But the dolphin perked its head up towards the couple. They were discovered. The dolphin raced towards the couple. The dolphin swam faster towards them, and they realized what it was when it got close. They could see it was a mermaid swimming towards them.

The extraordinarily beautiful creature got close to the couple, a little closer to Eric than to Andrea. Her beauty matched that of a goddess. The mermaid's hair flowed elegantly through the ocean's tides. Her face was sculpted with the beauty of the sea. Her skin looked like it was made of pearl, and her tail glistened red and green. The scales gave off a metallic shimmer that would catch anyone's eye.

She looked at Eric and smiled. "Hello travelers," she said, and turned to Andrea. "You must be wondering what you must do here. You see, I need your help. I can't find three of my most valued objects. They have been misplaced or moved by an angry fish. Will you please help me with this treasure hunt?" asked the mermaid.

Andrea and Eric looked at each other. They nodded in agreement and gave a thumbs up.

"Excellent! I was hoping you would say that. Okay, this is what I need. A green baseball bat, a red cooking pan, and a blue shovel. I need you to place them in those baskets over there. Can you do that for me? That would be delightful." The mermaid swam over and kissed them both on the cheek. She brought her hands up to her chin.

"Thank you so much. Let me sing you my song:

That puffer over there.

Give it a scare.

And it'll give you a breath of air."

She sang a melody, smiled, and swam off. Eric and Andrea picked up on the hint. They swam towards the puffer fish. His fins moved as quickly as lightning, but the puffer fish barely moved. The beak on him was sharp, and his wide eyes looked deeply into Eric and Andrea's. The fish swam steadily in place, but always looked at the couple. They were aliens to him. The puffer had to keep his guard up. He could not let them pass. Eric swam up to him. He got inches away from his face, and the puffer fish blew up like a balloon.

"Ha! Did you see that? He got scared when I got close. Wait, did I think that, or am I talking?" Eric asked Andrea. Andrea opened her mouth, but bubbles came out. "Can you hear me?" he asked. She gave him a thumbs up. "Holy shit, that puffer fish booked it. We gotta go find him again. Okay, let's just swim and see if we can spot him."

The couple went swimming towards a reef. They were relaxed. No monsters chased them. The water felt cool on their skin, and they could tell the sun was shining brightly above. The ocean floor beamed with energy and life. The coral had colors that didn't seem possible: oranges, purples, greens, and blues. It was as vibrant as a wonder. Andrea realized the coral was perfect camouflage for the objects they needed to find. The coral wasn't going to help, but she had to find that puffer fish. It would give the team an advantage.

Andrea set out to look for the puffer. It wasn't a glamorous fish; it was a little brown creature that hardly went quickly. It couldn't have gotten far. Or did it move it all? Andrea swam back to the original location of the puffer. There it was, swimming in place. Its fins were too small to generate any swimming power. It looked scared.

What is this puffer fish scared of? Odd, she thought to herself.

Andrea went up to the puffer fish. The water was calm around the fish. She approached the fish and reached her hand over his head. Andrea swatted down and waved in front of the puffer fish. It blew up like a balloon instantly. The puffer fish turned slowly and stared at Andrea. The fish was afraid; she could see it in his eyes. It looked deeply at Andrea with a stare of disgust and betrayal.

Andrea quickly became unnerved by the creature and swam towards Eric. Eric was searching in the coral for the puffer. He was enjoying the view and not really looking.

"Hey! I found it," Andrea yelled.

"You can talk now! Perfect! We have to find those objects. Do you remember what she said?"

Andrea stopped swimming and looked at Eric. "What is with you? Seriously. You forget everything."

Eric was stunned. He fumbled over his words. "I don't really know what to say. My memory fizzes out. Sometimes I don't want to remember things. I can try to work on it, but I can't get better at memory instantly, you know," Eric responded.

"Okay, fine, maybe it's not your memory. But please listen," Andrea told him.

Eric stopped to think about what she told him. He swam away to the reef. It curved in like a bowl. He sat in the water, floating and collecting his thoughts. Andrea figured he would be a while, sulking in his own mind.

The game isn't going to stop for Eric, Andrea thought to herself. *Hm, now what was it? A green baseball bat, a blue shovel, and a red cooking pan. I'm not sure about Eric sometimes. He has a lot of potential, but he hides under a fog of fiction.*

Andrea went out searching. She was entranced by the beauty of the coral. Little fish swam in and out of the coral like they were playing tag. All the fish were excited to be out. There was no barren coral to be found. That part of the ocean was thriving. Andrea kept swimming. She saw a twinkle on her right side. Her head turned slowly, and she scanned the area with her eyes, looking for the specific colors green, blue, and red. Her eyes separated all the colors in her field of view. All the other colors faded to gray. Her eyes fixated in one area that had a sparkle. Something was shimmering in the coral. The reef only had flat colors, but there was something shiny. It had to be metal, or clear. She saw the shine again.

Andrea located the source and swam towards the object. The shining got brighter. The red frying pan was within view. She was ecstatic. Andrea grabbed the pan and swam the object towards the red basket. The pan fell into the basket. Andrea was excited, but Eric was nowhere in sight. He had been swimming towards the bowl area of the reef when she saw him last.

Andrea swam next to the reef and noticed all the small fish swimming into the coral. It was not the same lively behavior they had had earlier. They were all fleeing into the cracks of the coral. A shadowy figure ran across the ocean floor. Andrea looked up quickly, but saw nothing. She thought it was Eric trying to play a prank on her. Eric was nowhere in sight, and her fear settled in.

Andrea stopped in her tracks. A presence in the water was felt. There was a chilling stillness underwater. If a cold electric current could pass through a body like a chill breeze, she felt it in her spine. The presence grew eyes. An intense glare pointed her way. She turned slowly and saw a small, dark, faded circle. It didn't look like anything she recognized. It floated in the distance. It did not move. It just stayed in one position.

"Move!" Eric screamed out. Andrea heard Eric, but she froze in fear. The dark circle was visible. Her eyes fixed on the object. Eric started swimming towards her as fast as he could. He flew through the water. Andrea didn't seem to notice Eric racing towards her. The circle started to get defined around the edges. The circle also got bigger. She knew that could only mean one thing: the object was getting closer.

Eric got to her just in time. He tackled her towards the bowl. She grabbed onto him when he made contact. The circle grew a line at the top. Her primordial instincts took over her nervous system. Something bigger, faster, and stronger was coming to eat her. Andrea nearly fainted. She held onto Eric tightly. A shark zoomed by where she had been waiting.

Eric took her into a small cavity of the bowl. He tucked her in closely. He looked at her and they stared at each other. Uncertainty made the waters turbulent. Andrea looked up at him. He raised a finger to his mouth to signal for silence. Andrea nodded sheepishly and knew Eric would keep them safe. An overhang was above them; it gave them protection from the overhead waters.

The shadow crossed the ocean floor. It looked like a submarine.

"What do we do?" Andrea said quietly.

"I have no idea; I think sharks are pretty keen on hunting things down," Eric said.

"Well, that doesn't exactly make me feel better," Andrea responded.

"Ah, well, you have to roll with it," Eric said.

"By the way, I found the red cooking pan."

"What? No way. Where did you find it?" Eric said excitedly.

"In the coral right over there, by the split."

"Wow, good job! That's honestly amazing. I'm sorry I had to take time to feel better. I just needed to process the things you said to me. It was a lot to take in, now that I listened to you," Eric said sorrowfully.

"No sense in beating yourself up now. I will accept your sorry excuse for an apology, but let's keep moving forward. This shark is really going to mess up our ability to explore freely. Baby, do you know if they have good vision?" Andrea asked sweetly.

Eric thought about Andrea's question. "I don't think they have the best vision. I think they can only see up close. Also, if you punch their nose, they get paralyzed."

Andrea looked at him slowly. "Do you honestly think you would punch a shark in the face?" Andrea questioned.

Eric thought. "Right now, I can confidently say yes, but if the shark was in front of me, I don't have an answer."

Andrea scoffed at Eric.

"Okay, so what's left on the list? You got the frying pan. I remember green and blue being the other colors," Eric said.

"Yeah, that's right. It was a green baseball bat and a blue shovel. We have to keep our eyes open for those objects. And avoid being eaten," Andrea said.

She realized that she was like the puffer fish: afraid, eyes open, anticipating an attack. Her nerves pulsated and her body was on high alert.

They had no idea how to get out of the situation. They stayed hidden under the cave. The missile-like shadow appeared on the ocean floor every once in a while. The shark circled above. Eric looked out into the distance; the sand was a very distinct yellow color, but he noticed a green outline sticking out of the sand.

"Hey Andrea, what do you think of that over there? It looks green and a little out of place."

Andrea stared in that direction. The shadow passed by again. She honed in on the area. Eric was right: something did seem off in the sand.

"I think you're onto something here. Should one of us go check it out?" Andrea looked at Eric.

"Yeah, I can do it. Can you be my eyes, though?"

"Of course. I will pop my head out and keep a lookout. I've started to recognize its patterns. It swims in a figure eight. There's going to be a time when it's swimming away from you. That's when you go in and try to grab the bat. Just bring it back here. There's no sense in you trying to find the buckets when I already know where they are," Andrea told Eric.

He agreed to the plan. It seemed like it would work. Andrea swam out slowly to the front of the cave. She swam up and looked for the shark. It was swimming away from them. "Just stay here for thirty more seconds. It just swam away from us. If we time it right, you can grab it and come back without it turning around," Andrea stated.

"Okay, let's wait it out. It can't be that much longer. I have patience."

The couple waited until they saw the shadow leave the area. Andrea swam up and saw the shark swim away. She signaled Eric to go get the item. Eric swam as quickly as he could to get to the bat. He kicked his legs hard and swung his arms forward, propelling himself forward yards at a time. He grabbed the bat with one hand, stopped himself from swimming, and tried to turn his body the other direction. Eric could see the shark swimming away. Eric felt confident the shark couldn't see him.

"I got it!" Eric called out, and swam back to their hiding nook. "How do you suppose we get the last one?" he asked.

"I will need time to think about that," Andrea responded. While Eric waited for her, he started to think of his own ideas, too. Eric thought if he could swim out and distract the shark, Andrea could have time to look over the ridge. But he figured she wouldn't think to send him into harm's way.

Andrea sat and thought. She knew the shark's pattern. The map was huge, and Andrea didn't want to assume things about her environment. The only place they hadn't been was the ridge. The shark swam too quickly for them to go and check the whole area. She looked for cover on the floor; they could try to evade the shark one bit at a time. There was some coral that looked tall with some dense sea anemone around it.

Which is the usual environment to camouflage? Andrea asked herself. It was possible the anemone could sting them. She looked at Eric and tapped him on the shoulder. Eric turned to her.

"You have any ideas? My idea is stupid. I would have to go out and distract the shark while you go searching along that ridge. It seems pretty risky to me," Eric said nervously.

Andrea sat there and thought about his plan. His plan would work, but she wouldn't want Eric to get caught by the shark.

"How about this: look at the far end of the reef over there. There are coral overhangs. They won't cover you fully, but check out the sea anemone. It's tall enough to hide in. We can both hide in there until the shark passes," Andrea said.

"I like the second idea a lot more than any of the other ones. I hope we can make it there in time," Eric said.

"I'm sure we will have plenty of time to make it. But we have to wait until the shark is right above us, and swim our asses off when it passes," Andrea responded.

The couple waited until the shark's tail was the last thing they saw. They darted towards the anemone. Both of them were able to hide successfully.

The anemone started to get very hot when the couple entered the cover at the same time. Eric stuck out his foot by accident. He realized it was much colder outside.

"Hey, I'm gonna swim out past the ridge to look for the last item. It's burning up in here!" he said. Andrea nodded. Once Eric had left the anemone, the heat went away. Andrea stayed behind, hidden. Eric swam quickly out to the opening past the ridge. There was something that looked out of place. He looked for the green baseball bat. Eric knew his time was running out. The shark would be making its rounds and scanning the area Eric was in. Eric searched some more before swimming back. The shark made its turn sooner than the couple had expected.

Eric swam as fast as he could towards the cave, but he was no match for the keen eye of a predator. The shark saw movement and swam faster towards Eric. Eric was swimming away when he caught a glimpse of the bat, right at the crest of the ridge. He thought he could swim towards Andrea to tell her. She was out of his way from escaping the shark. He thought it would be worth it and turned towards Andrea to shout, "The bat is right along the ridge! The floor!"

Andrea heard Eric scream out as he zoomed by with the shark on his tail. The shark had piercing black eyes. No sympathy came from the shark. It was just pissed off. Filled with homicidal rage, it was the apex predator. It followed Eric with ease. Any miscalculation on Eric's part and the shark would be inches closer.

Andrea saw this opportunity to go get the baseball bat. Without missing a beat, Andrea swam in the direction of the ridge. She scanned the floor ferociously. There was something off-colored in the sand. It did not match the jagged coral. This object was smooth and straight. Andrea swam faster towards the last object.

She reached down and grabbed it. Her swimming slowed to a halt and she turned to see what was happening.

Eric was out-swimming the beast. Andrea took that moment to dart towards the cave. Once she made it inside, she grabbed the red frying pan as well. She had both objects in her hands. Eric was too preoccupied with staying alive, and he hadn't noticed what Andrea was doing.

She rushed to the baskets. She swam over to the red basket and dropped the frying pan into it. Then she swam to the green basket and dropped the baseball bat into it. When the baseball bat hit the bottom of the basket, the shark had a spark go through him.

It slowed down, looked at Eric in disinterest, and swam away. Eric swam as if his life depended on it. Andrea let him swim a little while longer for her own amusement.

"Eric! You can stop swimming!"

Eric looked behind him and realized the shark had disappeared.

"Whoa, did I outrun it?" Eric said in surprise. Andrea slowly shook her head no. "What happened?" he asked.

"I swam over to get the baseball bat. I noticed the shark was still chasing you. Luckily, you swam the other direction, and I was behind you guys the whole time. I got the other object from the cave and dropped them both in the baskets."

Eric didn't let his ego get to him. He swam over to Andrea and hugged her. "Thank you. I was getting pretty tired."

"Looks like your plan worked after all, Eric," Andrea said with a smile, and quickly gave him a smooch on the cheek. Eric blushed; he was extremely lucky to have a woman like Andrea.

"C'mon, let's find the exit to this place before the shark comes back to take a bite out of you," Eric said.

The couple swam, doing quick flips and turns knowing their powers would soon disappear. A light emerged from the cave they were hiding in. To them, it seemed like the correct way to go. They swam deeper and deeper into the cave. The light got brighter the farther they went in. The surface of the water was right above them; a hidden tiny beach was inside the cave.

The couple gazed at its beauty. Stalagmites were everywhere in different colors. The rocks seem to be old and alive. The rocks had a personality to them. The door was in all of the rocks. It was a wooden door with yellow trim all around. The couple were used to opening doors, so they walked directly towards it without discussing anything.

CHAPTER 8: EMPIRES COLLIDE

The couple walked into a small room. It was all white. It looked like a hospital. It was small, like a closet. The couple had no idea where to go.

"I think we went the wrong way?" Eric asked.

"It's possible, but I feel like the machine is always guiding us. I feel like it wouldn't do that," Andrea said.

"The machine?" Eric said with confusion.

"Yeah, the machine. The one from the game show. It knew me in a way. It's been observing us, studying us, and it knows what we have and haven't done. I started crying after you froze. When it was my turn, it waited. It did not give me the question right away. It waited until I stopped crying and then asked the question. It's sentient. Crazy computers are running this whole place," Andrea exclaimed.

"Huh, that's really interesting. You know, I was skeptical about all those questions it kept asking. There must be cameras in here. Ha, I told you they were watching us," Eric said cheerfully.

"I really don't think we went the wrong way. We just have to look a little bit harder," Andrea said.

They searched the room together. They touched the walls and turned objects to see if something was a secret switch. Eric looked into a corner. He didn't know if his eyes were playing tricks on him or if he was really seeing things. The corner swirled into itself. It didn't make sense. The whole image was off. The lines never stayed in one place.

"Andrea, can you look at this? There is something off about this corner. Like, it's not staying still," Eric asked.

Andrea walked over to Eric to see what he was talking about. Andrea looked and noticed the same phenomenon.

"Whoa, that is trippy. Do you think it's real? Does the corner even exist? You should go inspect it," Andrea suggested.

Eric glanced over at her, but he knew she was right. She was not going to risk it.

"I don't want to get sucked in by anything. I would like to be warned first," Andrea explained.

Eric walked closer to the corner. He stuck his hand out towards the blurriness. His hand began to phase in and out. Eric let out a tiny yelp, worried about the existence of his hand.

"That was strange; my hand got all fuzzy. Like static. Like my signal was disrupted. That was a weird sensation. It looked like my hand was disappearing right in front of my face," Eric said with a quiver.

"Let me go closer and see what you mean."

Andrea stood by Eric. He stuck his hand out again, this time a little farther, up to his wrist. Eric's hand looked like it was glitching.

"It feels fuzzy, but it doesn't hurt. We should keep going."

Eric started to put his arm in. His hand disappeared altogether, and his arm pixelated out of reality. He shrugged his shoulders and stuck his head in.

Eric's entire torso vanished. His legs were stuck outside the portal with his feet firmly planted on the ground. Andrea covered her mouth in horror. Only half of her boyfriend was left, and not even the good half. She waited for him. She noticed he was wriggling until he finally popped back out. He had a huge smile on his face.

"It's badass. Oh my gosh, can we dive in, please? It's probably gonna suck us in. But I don't care, I want it to take me," Eric said with a boyish charm.

"Okay, calm down there. What is it?" she asked.

"It's nothing like I have ever seen. It's complete blackness at first. Suddenly, the lights around you start to get bright. And brighter. Galaxies start to unfold in front of you."

Eric had gained Andrea's curiosity. Eric had a dying curiosity about space. It did not give answers; only more questions. A person could spend a lifetime looking into the stars and only gain only an infinitesimal sliver of knowledge. Size seemed to lose meaning, and comprehending distance became the overarching challenge for three dimensional creatures bound by time. Eric smiled like a little schoolboy. Andrea appreciated how excited he got about his favorite subjects. He didn't get shy; he embraced his curiosity. She walked closer to the corner, grabbed onto the wall, and stuck her head in. Eric was right. It was pitch black at first. Slowly, light started to seep in. Stars shone from every direction. A galaxy appeared before her very eyes.

Andrea saw half of Eric's body sticking out. She looked over at him.

"Okay, yeah, we definitely need to do this one. Let's jump in!" Andrea said.

Eric heard her and they both hurled their bodies towards the portal. The couple went through the passage. They blasted off into a passing dimension. They moved faster in one direction. An unknown force pulled them in. Both of them looked at each other, swam towards one another, and clasped hands. It felt like they were in a tube. Inside of the tube was a conveyor of rolling purple felt.

Eventually, the couple saw a black dot appear in the very center of the tube. The black circle started to grow. The black circle enveloped them. They popped out like trash leaving a chute. The couple floated again. However, they could only move in a certain direction. It felt like a rope was attached to their hips. They walked in the only direction they were allowed. The couple realized they were floating in space. Trillions of stars surrounded them. A beautiful nova and cosmic patterns entranced them. Words appeared above that said, *Cosmic Skeeball.* The couple turned to each other and high fived. They were ecstatic about playing a game.

"Wow, this is a change of pace of how things were going. Skeeball seems so fun! I can't wait to play. It brings me back to playing at bars. Huh, I sure could use a beer right about now. That would be perfect," Andrea said.

"Some hops in space seem perfect? Haha, wow, what a thing to tell someone. 'I drank a beer in space,'" Eric replied.

"Yes! Exactly. Plus, I get better the more I drink in this game," she said with a smile.

Eric smiled at her and said, "Let's see what you got." He gave her a taunting expression with his face.

An invisible platform appeared under their feet. They noticed when their shoes hit a solid object. The couple got their footing and stood up. They had a perfect 360 degree view of all the stars. They started to walk farther up the platform. The couple noticed two machines sitting right next to each other.

The space underneath the machines glowed a subtle neon green. There were stairs in the shape of circles that led them to the machines. The bottom of every step in the stairs lit up when it was stepped on. Eric started to run up and down the stairs to see all the colors appear and reappear. Andrea rolled her eyes at him yet again.

There was a screen floating in space right above the skeeball machines. Andrea patiently waited in front of her machine until Eric was done playing on the stairs. Eric lost interest in the lights and noticed Andrea waiting at the machine and staring at him. He gave her a forced smile with his lips pressed together and stepped up to the machine. The stairs went dark and so did the machines. A white pulse came from the machines and flowed down the stairs, creating an elegant light pattern. The bottom stairs stayed lit. The pulses kept coming until all the stairs had light underneath them. The light stacked itself. Words started to appear on the screen.

The rules are simple. Play skeeball against one another. The first to 3000 points wins. No trick. Only treat. Both contenders continue to the final stage.

After reading the last sentence, the couple was shocked. They felt like the maze was going on forever. Their hopes were high with the end in sight. They were also super excited to play skeeball.

The lights dimmed and a blacklight was the only source of light. All the planets glowed fluorescent colors.

The couple was even more astonished than before. They felt good - better than good. Better than great, they felt like gods. They lived amongst the stars as the gods did. No one was in sight, and they had all the power and control.

The couple looked at each other. "You ready?" Andrea asked.

The ball fell on Andrea's side. No ball was given to Eric. A manual fell onto the ball. Andrea picked it up and read, "It is going to be a turn-based game with a lead of four-hundred to win after match point. This is to allow the second person to break the clinch and keep going."

"There's always something," Eric responded. His girlfriend picked up the ball and tossed it towards one of the holes in the middle. There was a handful of 100's in the middle, four 500 holes on the outside, and a 2000 in the very corner of the machine. Andrea hit 100 points. She jumped up and down.

Eric grabbed his ball. He looked up at the board to look at the points. *Wow, it's thirty rolls if I aim for those hundreds. But I could go for the five hundred and try to end it sooner. That two-thousand looks way too risky. But goddam, you can win in a couple of turns.* He thought all of this to himself.

Eric looked straight ahead. With fluid movements, he hurled the ball, banking it towards the left side. It went up, hit the barrier of the 500-point hole, and bounced out.

"Oh, c'mon, that was going in," he complained. Andrea let out a snicker towards him. He gave her a quick side eye. The ball rolled down to Andrea. She rolled 100 again. Eric rolled a 100 on his next turn.

"At this rate, it's gonna go forever. Also, one of us has to lose by four-hundred," Eric said.

"One of has to lose on purpose. Are you trying to make it easy for yourself?" Andrea said.

"Technically, that's the only way out. One of us must win. Ergo, someone must lose."

"I don't know, Eric; I want to win because I want to beat you. It looks like we're at an impasse."

"Yeah, and now you made us stuck," Eric scoffed.

"Oh, please. Give me a break. You love competition."

"Yeah, I do, Andrea. But I haven't been on a winning streak. You have seen it from my failed attempts these past couple of rooms. I ain't good right now; I have a bug."

"Pish posh, applesauce. I know you have that instinct in you. The instinct to be great. A couple blunders, sure. But you can come back from it. Just focus."

Eric took the words to heart. He sat there and thought about the simple things: breathing, being aware, and being present.

"Okay, I have a plan though," Eric said.

"Oh, do you now?" Andrea said, intrigued.

"We are not necessarily beating one another, but trying to accomplish the same goal. With the exception that one of us has to lose by a considerable number of points." Andrea kept nodding and following along. "I will only go for the two thousand. If I can get one of those and two five-hundreds, I can win. You can only go for the hundreds. But if I can't make any while you are at twenty-four-hundred I'll scratch the rest of my balls, so my score doesn't go up," Eric finished.

Andrea thought about it. She looked up into the sky, thinking. What would the universe tell her? Her finger rested on her chin.

"Sounds like a fair plan. Some competition sprinkled in with a common goal; I like that."

Eric nodded in agreement. He picked up his ball and aimed for the 2000. The ball went up and curved away from the hole. Eric missed his target by a wide shot. He looked at Andrea, who smiled and waved. She sank another 100. Eric looked fiercely at his targets and realized his shots were nearly impossible to make. He aimed for the 500. He threw his ball and it went into the 500 spot. It sank right in.

"Whoa! Hell yes," Eric shouted.

"Huh, you're onto something. We're almost tied. But if I can get to the two thousands, we will be coasting because I can finish the competition."

"Exactly!" Eric responded. Andrea smiled. Eric had come up with a good plan. She rolled her usual 100 points. Eric aimed for the 2000 again, but he missed. Andrea was catching up to Eric. Their plan only worked if someone lost by 400 points. Andrea rolled her 100, but missed! She looked at Eric and forced a sad face that she had missed. Eric shrugged his shoulders. It gave him an advantage.

Eric aimed for another 500. He sank it again. Eric has a considerable lead. Andrea even contemplated giving him the win, but that didn't sit right with her. She knew there was a chance she could beat him. It was Andrea's turn; she rolled the ball down the lane, but towards the 500 hole. Eric was a little confused. He looked at her. Her ball went behind the cage and missed the 500 by a hair.

"Hey, what happened? I thought we had a plan?" Eric asked Andrea.

"Hm, the plan works, but I kinda want to beat you. You know? I don't want to lose so easily." Andrea glanced at Eric with a goal in her eyes. It was on. Eric grabbed his ball and aimed for the 500, but missed.

It was Andrea's turn. She aimed for the 500 and made it cleanly through. Eric and Andrea were neck and neck. It was Eric's shot. He aimed for the 500 again and sank it. He took the lead, but not by much.

Andrea went for the 2000, but her ball didn't even get close to the hole. Eric's turn was up next. He went for another 500-point shot and he made it in. Two for two, he took a long stride into the lead. Andrea looked at him with a seething gaze. Eric wanted to gloat, but he knew that would end badly. He kept his cheers to himself. Andrea's facial expressions showed she was getting annoyed. She wanted to win; she was not happy.

"Okay, Eric, you may be winning now, but you will go down."

"Is that a threat or a promise?" Eric was smug. Andrea's nostrils flared. She picked up her ball and aimed for the 500. Her focus heightened and she honed in on the target. Every fiber of her being knew she was going to make the shot. Andrea walked up, tossed her hand back, and let the ball go at the end of her throw. It rolled down the alley. It popped up into the air perfectly towards the 500. It aimed straight towards the center until the very edge clipped the barrier guarding the hole.

Frustration took over Andrea. She stood quietly. Eric tried to get her attention, but she didn't turn.

"Hey, it's okay. We're going to get out of this. I just have to score more points," Eric said with a drifting silence. If fumes could have steamed off Andrea's head, they would have. Eric stayed quiet. The air was stiff, and he didn't want to make matters worse.

Eric grabbed the ball and aimed for the 500 but missed. He lost his streak of two and waited until the ball rolled in front of Andrea. He heard the thud of the ball when it contacted the wall. Andrea did not grab it immediately. Her stare was fixated on the cage. Time froze around her, and she stayed still. She nodded her head and grabbed the ball. The ball went towards the 2000-point hole. It grazed the surface of the alley. It flew into the air but leaned too far left and missed the designated target.

Andrea was disappointed nothing came from the throw. Her chances of coming back were very small. Every time she missed a 100, Eric's lead grew. She realized she should have stuck to the plan.

It was Erics' turn. He waited for the ball to roll down. He kept eyeing the 2000-point hole, but he didn't have the confidence to make it. He attempted a 500, but missed. It was Andrea's turn again. She rolled a 100 to be safe. She knew it was the smartest choice.

It was Eric's turn again. He thought about which hole to make. He had a strong lead, but wasn't close to the finish. The 2000 would be ideal, but it seemed like a pipe dream. It was too difficult. He had to go for the 500. He rolled and missed. The couple started to lose hope. A game they perceived to be enjoyable had turned against them. The constraints ruined the entertainment. But there had to be one victor. Andrea was getting long in the face.

The ball rolled down her alley, but she was losing motivation. Eric was beating her, and the plan favored him. It could have been a positive win for both of them. Andrea thought she could use the relief from carrying the team. She aimed for the 100 and made it.

It was Eric's turn, and he was getting sick of all the back and forth. He wanted to end the game, and he could see in Andrea's face that her interest in the game was diminishing, too. Once that was gone, morale would start to fall.

Eric grabbed the ball and clenched it tight. His knuckles turned white. The 2000 hole was locked in his eyes. He had it; he felt it. He knew what the ball felt like, he knew the weight, he knew the curve of the alley, and he knew the speed of the ball. He knew all the parameters to make this one shot. But could he execute it? His arm went back, winding up his throw. He took a step forward and released the ball. It zoomed down the lane. It popped up and hit the ceiling. The ball fell in the gutter.

"Ugh, goddammit, I overthrew the ball. We're going to be stuck here for a while."

"Stop being a sourpuss, Eric, it's not that bad. At least nothing is chasing us. Remember those times?"

"Yeah, I suppose. To be honest, it seems a little foggy. I know that happened, like with the shadow people. But it feels like a dream."

"I get you. We're not going to beat this stupid machine if we keep talking like this. Let's beat this thing."

"You got it!"

The couple started back up with Andrea's toss. Perfect. She made another 100. Consistency was key. It was Eric's turn. He felt relaxed. His hips were not tight. His arm was wiggly. His fingers had control. Eric tossed it down the track with finesse. The ball gently hit the alley. It arced beautifully in the air. He was on target. Eric hit the 2000 hole!

"Yes! Finally! Oh my gosh. Sorry babe, but I'm relishing this one for a while. Oh yeah. Yeah, this is awesome." Eric gloated by himself. Andrea stared at him, smirking.

"Oh my goodness, that was amazing, sweetie." Andrea clapped for Eric. He loved every second of the feeling of contributing and being a winner. His ego was big. It was hard to get that satisfaction. Not many men lived it.

"I'm so stoked, I killed it!" Eric applauded some more. The machine was excited; it raved with colors of joy. Patterns and strobes of light flashed in a joyous fashion. When Eric got louder, the intensity grew brighter.

Eric finally came back down to earth from his high. He knew they had to look for the way out of there.

The couple stepped down from the lofted platform. They looked for a door, as one would usually appear. Eric and Andrea enjoyed the view. They knew they would never experience anything like this in their lives again. They took a deep breath and let it all soak in. The cosmos was at their feet. They were titans of their little world. Things started to look up when Andrea spotted a blemish on the wall. Everything was pitch black, purple, and green. Beige was nowhere to be found, except in the tiny little spot. She saw it, tilted her head, and walked towards it. With her surroundings being fluorescent, the beige stood out. It didn't look normal. It looked out of place.

Andrea thought it would take her down the right path. Eric followed her instinctively. It looked like she was on the right track. She touched the beige spot; it was completely solid. Then she knocked on it.

Eric started getting closer and examining the beige dot. "Whoah, you saw this from over there? You've got eagle eyes or something. I can barely see it now," he said.

"I don't think I was looking for it. It jumped out at me. It didn't match anything it was next to. But the question is, what do we do to get into the next room?" Andrea asked.

Eric scratched his head. The couple started to think together. He walked over to the wall and stuck his hand through the beige spot.

"Whoa, there's another side."

Eric grabbed the edges of the beige spot. It had an outline, and its ridges were solid. It was a hole. He grabbed the edges and pulled open a perfectly cut-out square from the entire universe. It acted like a doorknob to their next room. Eric and Andrea walked through the entrance to continue the game.

CHAPTER 9: POSITIONS

They entered the last room. Glowing red lines shone through the cracks of white, hexagon-shaped tiles. The ceiling stretched farther than the eye could see. The tiles were huge; one tile could fit a whole car on its surface. The room had white walls and glowing lights all around. As opposed to the other rooms, this one looked very futuristic. Chrome accents were all over. It added an extra touch of style. They walked closer to the middle of the room.

The ground started to shake and brought the couple to their knees. The floor panel shook violently and lifted off the ground. The panel levitated in the sky. It was cone-shaped, and at the bottom was a little jet engine. The jet nozzle rotated and allowed the panels to fly across the room. The panels beneath the couple separated and flew them to different sides of the room.

Eric tried to grab hold of Andrea, but the tile flew away rapidly. Andrea reached her hand out, but it was too late to grab Eric's. She barely grazed the tip of his finger. The couple was torn apart one more time. They looked into each other's eyes as the pieces flew away in their own direction.

Eric's perception of the room changed as he flew higher. He noticed a dark corner where a small, bright sign was posted. The sign was too far away to make out any of the words. He saw the corner again and it looked like a door. It looked like an emergency exit. It looked too good to be true.

"Hey Andrea! Can you see that sign over there? It's behind you, to the right." Eric grabbed her attention. She looked behind her to see what he was talking about. She saw the floating green sign. It read, *Exit.* Andrea knew with all her heart that this was the way out. This was the last room. They had to defeat the machine one last time.

There was only one other door in the room: the exit. Andrea and Eric looked at each other from afar. The tiles on the ground settled down in a certain configuration in front of them. There were noticeable gaps on the floor. Most of the gaps were too wide to jump across. The couple looked at where their tiles had taken them. They each had a brightly glowing, multicolored control panel at their side. There were buttons, handles, and switches, but none of them were labeled.

Eric, the more curious of the two, pushed a square green button. A loud sound came out and an intense buzzing flooded their ears. They quickly raised their hands to their ears to stop the sound. Eric quickly pushed the button again and the ringing stopped.

"I think all these buttons do different things! Push the green button!" Eric yelled across the room.

Andrea looked at the control panel and pushed her green button. The ceiling opened like a trap door, and a bright white light came beaming down as if God were looking at the two. The light was too intense to even look at. They both closed their eyes and succumbed to the force that took away their vision. Andrea tried her best to shield her eyes and find the green button again.

She was blind and hit the button next to the green one. It was a yellow one. The ground started to shake, and the tiles started to change configuration. The pattern when they first entered the room disappeared. Andrea looked over, barely peeking her eyes through the slits of her fingers, and pressed the green button. The two halves of the ceiling closed, and the light disappeared.

The couple removed their hands from their faces and looked out. "It looks different! The floor I mean," Andrea shouted to Eric.

"I think you're right! Did you press something?"

"I pressed a button by accident when the light blinded us! I thought it was the green one!" Andrea said.

"We have to make a path towards that door over there!" Eric replied.

The couple took time to examine their control panels. Eric looked at his and noticed two big levers at the top. He looked over his shoulder and stared at

Andrea's. Andrea's panel did not have the same levers at the top. He thought about how difficult this room might be. But he was happy to have Andrea back to help solve the puzzle. She was the brains of the group and he knew it.

Andrea did the same. Her panel had a unique blue dial. She looked at Eric's, and his did not have any dials. She knew this was going to be tricky if the panels did not mimic each other. She wondered if all the buttons did something different on each panel. Andrea looked at the door and there were no tiles underneath it.

Looking at the door, she hoped it was the last one. Andrea was getting tired, hungry, and a bit irritated, but thought that it was a fun experience overall. And most importantly, she was with the man of her dreams. She could be trapped in a well with him and would know everything would work out.

Instead of looking at his panel, her gaze went to him. Andrea admired him; Eric wasn't the sharpest tool in the shed, but there was a spark in him. Driven by life itself, he never had dull moments. He made any situation into a great experience. That was what she loved most about him: his energy propagated. It helped that he was a handsome fellow. While Andrea was looking at him, Eric turned around and smiled.

"Any ideas on how to do this?" he asked.

"Yeah, I've been giving it some thought. I feel like we're gonna have to try most of the buttons and see what they do. One of them must lead us to that door over there." Andrea pointed to the wall.

"I like that idea; we should take notes on which buttons do what. We know what three of them do, at least," Eric said.

"Tell me exactly what your panel has, then," Andrea replied.

Eric nodded. "Okay, the first one was that green button with the high-pitched sound. It's in the middle of a group of buttons that are all different colors. It looks like a square. There are four buttons on each side with the big green one in the middle. The rows are all different colors. The left side is yellow, the right side is purple, the top is blue, and the bottom is red. But it's interesting that the corners are black ones."

"Okay, keep going!" Andrea yelled.

"There are two huge levers on the right side. They look cartoonish, like the ones used to shut off all power. The left side has two buttons. One is a red circle, and the other is a checkered square one. That's all of them."

"I'll tell you mine then. The first one I hit was that green one. By accident, I hit the yellow one. All the buttons are in a line. Huh, they are all different colors. The first is red, and following to the right is orange, green, blue, indigo, and violet. It's the whole rainbow! Okay, to the right of those are two big dials, and it looks like they make a full rotation. To the left is a trackpad. It looks like my finger can draw on it," Andrea told Eric.

Eric sat on the floor, thinking. "So, my panel has fifteen buttons and two levers. While yours has seven buttons, two dials, and a trackpad. It might take us a while to figure out what all these do. "First, we will figure out what all the buttons do and get to that second lever. I'm going to push one of the black ones," Eric said.

"Go for it." Andrea braced against the wall and waited for something to happen. Eric pushed the black one in the corner.

Nothing happened.

"That was odd. I wonder if they forgot to connect those?" Eric asked.

"Try the other black ones," Andrea said.

Eric pushed the other black buttons, but nothing happened when he pressed them. "They're probably just dummy buttons. There might be a couple on yours too."

"I say we keep messing with yours first and figure it all out before mine. There could be an order we have to push them in. Not only do we have to find the correct buttons, it's possible they have sequence. Hey, do you see a hint anywhere?" Andrea asked.

The couple started looking at the panels, floor, and walls. At first, they did not notice anything. Eric kept looking at the control panel. He saw a small handle that he didn't notice before. He pulled up the hatch and the hint appeared: *AI is strong, but humans must be stronger. Computers rely on sensors just as humans rely on their senses.*

He read it aloud to Andrea. "Does yours have a small handle?" Eric asked. Andrea found one as well. The hint read, *Physics or no physics, this room prefers the latter.*

Andrea started talking. "Like always, they don't really give us an answer. But your hint gave us more of a clue. I think we're trying to beat the computer, like chess."

"Ugh, I hate chess! There are way too many pieces and moves! If you are comparing the room to chess, do you think the computer has a chance to take a turn after we do something?" Eric stated.

"I'm not sure, but there's only one way to find out: we keep on playing. Let's try to hurry. I'm starting to get tired. I wish we were back in your apartment, cuddling in bed." A sadness fell over Andrea. Eric saw it in her face. He wanted to console her, but there was no visible path to her.

"The first thing I am going to do when we are next to each other is give you a big bear hug and all the kisses," Eric said in a soft, soothing voice. Andrea had the biggest smile on her face.

The couple was determined and motivated to beat the machine. They were united. Eric and Andrea had a common enemy. They banded together to form a team that could take on any entity.

"Eric, keep pulling more levers to see what they do. Or try that big red circle one. It looks interesting."

Eric looked at it. It was glossy and shiny. It looked forbidden, like a button that should only get pushed in emergencies, when everything had reached a state of chaos and the button was the last hope for restoring order. The button glistened, and he hoped it had a good tactile feel to it. It was always disappointing to push a button with no resistance. It should be stiff and mechanical; a satisfying click to finish the stroke.

Eric pushed the button. Once it was fully compressed, he let go. The couple's anxiety started to rise. An electrical whirring sound emerged from the ground. It got louder, and the intensity increased. Bright red lasers started to shine from the corners of the hexagonal tiles.

The lasers formed a grid above the couple. The grid was composed of empty spaces and tiles. They had no discernible features or patterns, but they clearly established the boundaries of the map.

"What do you think it is, Andrea? It kinda looks like a map or a course. You know?"

Andrea understood Eric. "But what do you think we're supposed to do with it? It's not really giving us a direction. More of a limitation of where we can go. Do you think these lasers are dangerous?" Andrea asked Eric with concern.

"Hm, I'm not too sure; it would depend on how strong they are. I will test the waters," Eric told Andrea. She had a confused look on her face as she waited to see what he would do. He took off his shirt. Andrea was pleasantly surprised.

"Hey, put it back on!" she yelled out to him.

"No, hold up, it's part of my plan." Eric grabbed his shirt and wrapped it around his hand. He grabbed onto a ledge and reached out as far as possible to get the shirt to touch a laser. His arm stretched out all the way. A hiss came out when the laser made contact with the shirt. Eric saw smoke emerging from the laser. He retracted his shirt. His sleeve had burst into flames. A small cry was let out by Eric. Andrea saw the commotion and had a chuckle. Eric grabbed his shirt, threw it to the ground, and stomped on it.

A small hole had appeared with black, burnt edges. He gasped with sadness.

"Jesus, your shirt caught on fire. Haha, put it on and we will see how bad it is."

Eric grunted, "Okay, fine."

Eric grabbed the shirt by the sleeves and rolled it over his head. Eric adjusted the fit and pulled the shirt down. His shirt was wrinkled and stiff. Eric lifted his arm to get a better look at the ruined part. On his left sleeve, there was a small hole with singed edges.

"Aw, c'mon, I just bought this shirt. Now it's ruined. I like the way it fits, too." Eric was sad his shirt couldn't be worn anymore.

"At least it didn't happen in the beginning. We're almost done, and I can get you a new shirt. Besides, it looks cool once you get past the whole 'escaped a fire' look." Andrea smiled at Eric.

He chuckled. "I guess it is kinda cool. Okay, but these lasers just made it harder for us to get across the other side. I don't want to fall or touch the lasers. I'd rather not have my skin melted off the bone. I'm not ready for that kind of thing," Eric said.

Andrea kept looking at the grid. She thought it was interesting. It made a perfect grid, but she couldn't tell. Andrea was too low. She had to gain a good vantage point to get a good look at it. There was a small column to climb up. The top of the tower was easy to get to. Once Andrea looked down, she said, "Ah ha."

"What do you see?" Eric asked.

"I think it's a board. Like a board game. Each floating tile is in each square."

Eric decided to look for himself. He found a wall to climb and looked towards the lasers. "Huh, what do you know? It is like a grid. I hope it's like Battleship. Maybe we're supposed to sink all the floating platforms? It would be fun to see some shit blow up. Even better would be launching missiles!"

"I think you're getting ahead of yourself there, babe. Let's see what the other buttons do. I sure hope it's battleship," Andrea told Eric. Eric smiled from ear to ear, waiting for one of the platforms to blow up into a million pieces.

Andrea was curious about the trackpad and started to touch the screen. She moved her finger across it and a weird noise started to hum. The humming got stronger every time she rubbed her finger across the pad. She slowed down and went the opposite way. The same hum sounded. When she let her finger go, Andrea gasped and heard a clunk in the background, like two gears grinding to a halt. When she turned, she saw nothing. Eric wasn't paying attention when she looked at him. He was pretending to be in a spaceship. He pretended to put a walkie talkie to his mouth and started to point at things. It looked like he was giving out commands.

"Looks like I'm alone on this one," Andrea said under her breath. Andrea placed her finger back on the pad. The source of the noise couldn't be located. Her finger moved along the middle. Nothing changed or moved from her angle.

"Whoa, check it out. One of the pieces is moving!" Eric called out. Andrea let go of the pad, but a wall obstructed the view.

"Oh, never mind, it stopped," Eric told Andrea.

"Wait, keep looking at that piece. I am going to try something." Andrea ran back to the track pad. She slid her finger across the top, and the humming came back.

"There it goes again; it's moving! It looks like it's on some sort of track. It could only move on its track! When you get the chance, you should look."

Andrea stopped moving her finger and went to look at the track Eric was talking about. The track started on the side Eric was on. The other side of the track led nowhere. Strange.

"Move it over here so I can jump on it!" Eric yelled out.

"Wait, no, not yet. You have no idea where that thing goes. Look at the end. There's no place to go at the end of the track," Andrea responded. Eric put his hand over his eyes to clear his vision. She was right: the platform led to a horrendous fall.

"Okay, yeah, I see what you're saying."

Andrea stood back up and looked at the pad.

Eric was getting curious. He wanted to see what the other buttons could do. It was possible something miserable would happen if he activated them. He didn't want to catch Andrea off guard.

"Hey, I'm going to push another button. It may help or hurt us, but we won't know until we activate it," Eric yelled out to Andrea.

"Yeah, that sounds fine. I'm ready."

Eric looked down at the buttons, but he didn't know which one to choose. He went with the button that looked the most appealing. The checker-patterned button looked appealing, and he pressed it. Noises sounded from underneath. More floating platforms flew to the inside of the squares. The couple looked at the new additions.

Eric raised his eyebrow up. "That looks promising."

Andrea looked at her panel, and she noticed the two big dials on the side. She was curious about what they were capable of. The left dial was closer to Andrea, and she turned it. A chill spread through her body. Everything seemed to grow dark. Frost appeared on metal surfaces. She could see the breath in front of her face like it was a winter night. Eric shivered.

"Hey, it got pretty cold in here. Or am I going crazy?" Andrea asked Eric.

"It definitely got chilly," Eric replied.

Andrea looked at the dial again and turned it in the opposite direction. The room grew bright, and it felt like heat lamps were turned on full blast. It dawned on her. "Oh, this dial must control temperature." She looked at the other dial and turned it. It went completely dark.

"Ah! I lost my vision!" Eric yelled out. Andrea looked around and saw nothing. Flashbacks of losing her vision in the deer room came back. She turned the dial back, and the lights turned on.

"Oh wait, never mind. It just went dark," Eric said.

Andrea didn't mention she was changing the temperature and the lights. Her buttons controlled the environment. She could make it as cold as a tundra or as scorching as sand dunes. Andrea saw the power she had. The power to take over someone's environment was overwhelming. Controlling a person's environment could change their actions. She saw similarities between that power and the machine.

Andrea messed with the temperature and the lights before she told Eric because his reactions were humorous. He didn't know what to make of it. He looked down at his buttons and looked for another to press. One of the purple buttons looked delightful, so he gave it a press. The walls started to make strange sounds. The ceiling tiles shifted and exposed two gas pipes. He wondered what was going to come out of the tubes. A hissing sound filled the room. Green smoke flowed out of the openings and sank to the ground.

"That's not good. Andrea, look up!" Eric screamed out.

Andrea looked up towards the ceiling. She saw the concerning situation. "Just hold your breath for now!" Andrea shouted. The couple tried holding in as much oxygen as possible until the smoke cleared. A few seconds passed by, and Eric let in a big gasp.

"I can't do it! It's too much pressure." He started to breathe the surrounding air. The green fog had reached the floor, where it hovered next to his feet.

"Hahaha! I don't know why, but this floor is the slickest floor ever. Hahah ha ha. Oh my gosh, if I were a seal, I would be rockin' this shit." Eric blabbered. Andrea had her mouth shut. Her eyes focused on Eric. She was in shock.

What has gotten into him? He's wandering around like a fool, and he's blurting out nonsense, she thought to herself. Andrea kept holding her breath. The gas eventually stopped. Eric was having a blast giggling at something involving TNT, a fake tunnel, and a very dumb wolf. Andrea couldn't hold her breath for much longer. Her mouth opened and she took a deep breath.

The smoke hit the back of her throat; it was a thick, dense vapor. She started to giggle. Laughing took over her senses. Andrea pointed and looked at Eric.

Eric noticed Andrea looking at him. His mouth opened wide and his eyes squinted hard. He fell on the floor, laughing and rolling around. He couldn't believe it. He saw her. She laughed harder seeing him fall on his back. They laughed until their sides hurt. The laughter slowed down. The couple got back to their senses. Eric chuckled.

"Whoa, what do you think that was?" Eric asked Andrea.

"I have no idea. You looked like a complete idiot."

"I couldn't help it. It just came over me. I couldn't control it. I started to laugh, and then I couldn't stop laughing. One thing led to the next and everything in my head was funny. But the best part was when I saw you breathe it in. Once I looked into your eyes, I knew. I had a great time, though. Huh, what if it was laughing gas?"

Andrea looked at Eric and she started to nod. It made sense.

Eric looked back at the panel; all the purple buttons were turned off. Andrea looked at her panel and saw the red button. She went over to the console and pushed the button. Sound started to emerge from the bottom again. The ground shook, nearly knocking Andrea off balance.

A structure emerged from the floor. A long white pillar shot up from the bottom. Fins stuck out of the pillar. They looked like blades with a little curvature. They resembled hot air balloons. It came flying up between the path of the grid and some other platforms. It violently shoved platforms out of the way. The structure had a big base and tapered upwards. Once the full structure stopped moving, the blades started to spin at a relatively slow speed. Everything finally settled into place. It looked like a giant windmill.

"Are we gonna talk about that weird spinning thing in the middle?" Eric asked.

"There's not much to say. It's out of the way. Who knows? It's not in our path. I don't think we should worry about it too much for now," Andrea responded. Eric agreed with Andrea.

She looked at the next set of buttons that gained her interest. The yellow one caught her eye. It looked like a yellow gumdrop made of pure sugar and lemon. She pressed it. Whirring and buzzing noises started to come from the dashboard.

The whole console started to move and reconfigure. The console was all electro-mechanic. The machine looked organic in the way it moved its own pieces. Andrea saw a map materialize in the air. Tiny glass particles suspended in space. Light bounced off the shimmering planes. It formed a three dimensional image of a map.

Andrea saw herself and Eric represented by two red dots. "Whoa, Eric. One of my buttons gave me a map, and I can see both of us on it. There's even depth. It's a really big help, I think. Move around a little bit!"

Eric listened and ran to different sides of the platform. Andrea was astounded that the dot followed him perfectly.

"Hey, this is really helpful. I can't see where you're going from this angle. I can also see all of the platforms," Andrea told Eric.

"Yeah, I agree. There's something we need to activate to complete the maze."

Eric looked at his panel again. The yellow button was lit up. Eric pushed the yellow button and waited for something to happen. Metal clicked together and mechanisms became active. One of the platforms had a patterned movement. It slid to one side, paused, then slid to the other side. It paused on both ends. Eric wanted to see where the path led. He climbed on top of a pillar and saw past the trail.

The moving platform paused right underneath the giant windmill. The windmill had a small opening at the bottom where the platform stayed. Eric knew he was going to have to jump through. The acrobatics needed to make the jump successfully were incredibly difficult.

He was worried about his capabilities. Eric decided not to think about it, because it might not be a part of the game. The blue button had a shiny metallic finish. It looked like it was taken off a brand new car's paint job. His finger pushed the button down into the panel. A hissing noise started up. Eric freaked out and looked frantically to see where it was coming from. There was a blank wall, and a light had appeared on it. Eric could see the source of the hissing. Two big hydraulic pistons lifted a panel from the wall and revealed a big plever. It was a huge lever that was wider than a couple of feet. Eric observed the new lever, and he noticed two small buttons on the floor next to it.

"Hey Andrea, come take a look at this giant switch!" Eric pointed in the direction of the new lever.

"I see it! Let me look at the map to see if we can get to it." Andrea saw the lever on the map. It was shown by a pale blue dot, but Andrea couldn't find a path that led towards it.

"Hey, this is going to sound strange, but right now it's impossible to get there," Andrea told Eric.

"What do you mean?"

"It is physically impossible for us to get over there. There are no bridges or platforms, so right now there's no way we can get to that platform. Unless we can fly again"

Eric jumped up to see if he could fly. Sadly, it was to no avail. Eric returned back to the ground.

"All of my buttons are pushed! There is nothing that could help us over here," Eric said.

Andrea heard him and looked at the buttons she had to press. Andrea looked down the row of colors. She thought the orange looked pretty and pushed the button. Andrea did not hear or see anything. Andrea started to wonder whether the button had a function at all. Before she pressed the next button, a shriek came from behind. She looked over in Eric's direction. He faced a wall. It seemed like something Eric would do, and she didn't think much of it. However, he swayed back and forth, so she figured something was up.

"Whatcha looking at?" Andrea asked.

"You're not going to believe this. I can see through walls. It's not too interesting. I can only see, like, wires and ducting. It's not exciting at all. Unless..." Eric stared at Andrea. He tried to lock her into his vision.

Andrea noticed him staring. "Uh, what are you doing? Ew, you creep. Knock it off."

Eric kept looking at her with a smile on his face. "Yeah, it totally doesn't work; I can't see anything," Eric told Andrea. She shook her head in disappointment.

"C'mon, focus. We need to get out of this maze. Who knows · this could be the very end."

Eric agreed with Andrea. She looked at the next available buttons. There was one that looked like a purple pill. Andrea walked over and pressed it directly in the center. Loud bangs erupted from underneath. The floor and map shifted again. Andrea and Eric fell to their knees. They gripped anything within arm's reach.

Eric's platform raced off into a corner and made a hard left. Eric hung onto a pole for dear life. He looked like a flag waving in the wind, and Andrea was terrified. If he let go, he would fall down to the bottom. The floor was not visible, so who knew how far the drop was? It'd be a long, tormenting fall · a fall Andrea did not want Eric to go through.

She yelled encouraging words for him to grip harder. Eric heard her and made his knuckles turn white. The platform slowed down to a halt. Eric finally regained his balance. He looked at Andrea in confusion and was deeply scared.

Andrea looked at her map. Some of the platforms had moved to different locations. Luckily, they moved in spots that gave the couple an advantage. New crystals formed on the map. She looked across the landscape and saw a path towards the lever.

Eric looked to see where the tiles had moved him. He looked at the new path, but there were obvious gaps that were longer than a jump. The big windmill was up ahead. It was a huge obstacle in his way.

"Hey, Eric! I think I have something for you!"

He looked up at Andrea. Her hand was on a switch. She pulled it down to activate it. Platforms rose up to the level Eric was on. The two tiles moved in a circle around pillars. Each rotated in unison with the other. If he timed it correctly, he could jump across both of them to make it across to the other side.

"Hey Andrea, how does it look on the map? These tiles keep spinning. I don't know which one to jump on. The big windmill thing is going to be in my path. Can I get to the door or the lever from here?"

Eric was curious and nervous. He did not want to mess this up. He recalled all the mistakes he had made during the maze. Failing some of the rooms gave Eric a burden. He had to focus on the main goal: to finish the maze.

"Okay, I looked at the map! A couple of pieces are still missing. They are way too far apart for you to jump across. I have to pull more levers and push more buttons. Are there any new buttons for you?" Andrea questioned.

"Nope, nothing over here. After the map readjusted its terrain, all of my buttons stopped working. The only thing I can think of is that far-away lever," Eric told Andrea.

"Oh, you're totally right - I forgot about that new one. Okay, let me double check the route. Give me a second." Andrea observed the map. Her finger pointed at Eric's little red dot and traced it to the lever. The route would work, but it needed one more tile to complete the path. There were so many buttons and levers. It felt intimidating to have so many choices, and she hoped to find the correct one.

Andrea stared at the empty gap that was in Eric's path. There was a green, halo-shaped light in the gap. Her brow furrowed, and she figured she should look back at the panel of buttons. There was a light green button that matched the color of the halo. Andrea gave it a press.

There was movement around her platform. One of the tiles had moved out of the way and into another spot! The tile switched positions and made a path for Eric.

Eric used his new X-ray vision. When he stared at the pillars, they were only an outline that he could see perfectly through. The tiles that moved had an extensive wiring layout. The wires glowed yellow. The moving tiles looked like a golden bird's nest. All the wires were jumbled in a circular pattern, unlike the stationary tiles, which were hollow.

He figured the tiles that moved were his best option to reach the lever. Eric saw two tiles that were stationary and off to the side. They both had wiring harnesses on the inside. He tried to remember those; it was possible they could help them finish the maze.

Andrea was getting flustered at all the available choices. She didn't want to make a mistake, no matter how small it was. There was a big blue button off to the side. It had a red dot in the middle, with other dots in a circle. It resembled a firework. The button persuaded Andrea to press it. There were no loud noises from machines.

She looked at her arms to make sure nothing had happened to her. Nothing had happened, and she felt normal. Andrea heard a scream and looked over to Eric.

He was frantically running away from a machine. It was a giant spinning platform with laser cannons on the sides. Lasers were shooting out in different colors. The lasers shot plasma at an extreme velocity. The menacing device chased Eric.

"What the hell is this thing! I can't outrun it, it's too fast!" Eric was barely able to escape its wrath. Quick cuts allowed Eric to get ahead of the machine. The mechanical monster was fast, but it could not turn as quickly as Eric. Laser shots were getting closer to Eric's ankles, nipping his heels more with every second that passed. One laser hit his heel. His shoe went flying off. He stumbled a little, but was able to regain his balance.

"Oh my gosh! That was my mistake!" Andrea yelled out to him. She had to fix the situation she had put Eric in. The blue button she pressed had grown a steel cage around it. The button could no longer be touched.

Andrea panicked and saw a handle on her console that appeared. There was a tiny diagram next to the handle that looked like three roman columns. Andrea thought it was worth a try. She grabbed the handle and turned it. It was tough to turn and very rigid. Once it turned a quarter of a rotation, a satisfying click sounded off. It locked in place and sank into the panel.

Andrea heard machinery move. She looked at the map to see if there were any changes. Big pillars emerged from the depths of the chamber. They erected next to Eric. She could see him running. Anguish sank into her body. She wanted to protect Eric and keep him safe, but she had put him in a predicament. Andrea started studying the map.

"Things just keep getting worse for me," Eric said under his panting. "Andrea! These giant towers came out! And a killer laser dreidel! I think they are sniper towers! They're going to start shooting at me! I don't think I have enough agility or stamina to live!" Eric was worried. He stayed on the tiles and ran to avoid getting shot.

"I have something for you! But you have to listen and follow the plan."

"Anything is better than what I am going through right now. And make it sooner rather than later!"

"Okay, hear me out. You're doing great avoiding the spinning laser. When I look at the map, the laser machine can't keep up with your sharp turns. It's too big, and the spinning slows it down. Try to cut in the opposite direction it's rotating. It'll buy you more time."

Andrea paused and heard a noise approach from behind. It was a dark presence. Andrea got goosebumps, and chills ran down her spine. She heard linkages move. Andrea turned around to see what was happening. A new door had opened.

Two little pixies flew out. Andrea had to do a double take. The pixies flew around together. Little sparkles shimmered off of them. They were both girls, and they giggled while they flew. The girls had wands that they waved around. Andrea stared at the pixies until they noticed her. Andrea froze. She didn't know how they would react to her. The colors of the pixies changed to a crimson red. They zoomed right by Andrea's face. She stepped back and tried to swat at them.

"Those bitches."

Anger flowed through Andrea, and she tried swatting them away. It didn't deter the fairies from flying close to her face. One of the pixies stopped in front of Andrea's face. The pixie was so close that Andrea went cross-eyed. The pixie flicked its wrist and shot a little poof of glitter at Andrea. The glitter zipped right to her nose and dispersed into smoke. Andrea shook her head and sneezed violently.

"That's annoying."

The pixies laughed in the sky together and kept flying next to Andrea's head.

"What's going on? I could use the help!" Eric called out. He didn't get a response and thought Andrea had her hands full as well. The towers were the closest objects. Nothing bad was coming out of the towers and they appeared to be safe, unlike Eric had thought. The laser grid shone with intensity in his X-ray vision.

The machine flew above the grid. Eric figured the machine could not go through the grid. It was a pleasing thought that the destroyer couldn't smash into him. He ran closer to the pillars. Eric was able to maneuver around the pillars. The machine made a low-pitched hum. It slowed down. Eric could not believe it. The machine spun to a halt. It spooled up and changed direction. Eric knew he could keep the machine at a distance with his agility. His only concern was outpacing it and being in a vulnerable position.

Andrea kept swatting away the little beasts. When the door to the pixies had opened, a new button had popped up from the console. It was a thin, aluminum bezel with a spotlight shining up from it. She went to the lit-up button and tried to stick her hand in it. There was no reaction. Nothing happened to her hand when she removed it from the light. A pixie splashed dust on her and made Andrea sneeze. She wiped her face and waved her hand above the light. A tile ran across the map.

"That was interesting." She raised her hand and gestured in the other direction. The tile went the other way. She raised both hands, and two tiles zoomed across the map. She pulled in her hands, rotated her palms, and looked at them. Moving the tiles felt telepathic. Andrea played with the tiles, making them move past each other in a criss-cross pattern. She got distracted by the light, and one of the pixies nailed her in the face with dust. Andrea let out an obnoxious sneeze.

"Just my luck. There are tiles flying at me now! I have to avoid those tiles, too," Eric said. He slowed down and kept the machine turning in different directions.

"Eric, I'm moving those pieces! Sorry, little fairies came out and they're messing with me. I'll try to move the tiles into a good place for you." Andrea scanned the map, looking for a tight corner the machine had to turn into. She picked a spot between two pillars. Eric saw the moving tiles. A blip of inspiration came out as he stared at the levitating platforms.

"Can you move two of the tiles on the same pillar to make them gog up like a staircase? I'm gonna need your precision. I want to jump -" The machine came up behind Eric and shot lasers that got close to hitting him. Eric ducked and turned into the pillar.

"I am going to jump up using the two tiles and jump down the pillar on the other side. I am going to need you to swing the other tile around so I can land on it when it's under me."

"I got it."

Eric took a deep breath and sprinted down the middle to gain space between him and his enemy. Andrea swirled her hands in an elegant movement and placed the tiles. The platforms wrapped around the pillar, one above the other. Eric saw his opening and made a quick turn to his left. The first tile approached. He jumped up and grabbed the first tile. The jump didn't get him to the platform. His chest hit the side and Eric grasped onto a pipe on the floor. He hung by a thread. The machine turned the corner and started to gain speed at Eric. The humming of the machine got closer. Eric pulled himself up onto the platform and jumped to the next one.

Andrea looked at the map and saw his dot jump onto the second platform. She moved the other tile underneath Eric. He waited until the machine was right above him. When the machine had gotten on top of Eric, he jumped down to the lower platform. His foot twisted and he fell to the floor. The destroyer followed Eric downwards.

The machine collided directly into the lasers. The metal singed and burned, and panels flew off the giant laser unit. Sparks emitted from every corner. The wounds of the lasers had completely torn apart the machine. It lost its capacity to fly and plummeted to the floor, where it collided with a pillar. The tile exploded into a fiery ball. Eric lay on one of the platforms Andrea controlled. It unexpectedly flew across the map. Eric almost fell off the tile before he could grab onto a ledge.

Andrea tried to swat away one of the pixies. She unintentionally scooted Eric across the map.

"Whoops, sorry again, baby!" Andrea apologized.

It put Eric into a good position; one of the walkways was within range for Eric to jump on. Eric walked on the straightaway and recognized one of the features. The spinning tiles had a specific pattern. They were in sync. The tiles moved together like two cogs meshing.

Eric timed it. He bounced his head up and down, counting the beats. The sweet spot appeared, and he ran towards the platform. His foot landed on one of them, so he kept moving forward. Eric immediately jumped onto the other one. The tiles were like a hopscotch pattern, and he jumped onto them easily. One last leap off the rotating platforms, and he landed on a straightaway.

He stood up and looked ahead. Eric saw the massive obstruction. The windmill structure had wings that spanned across a third of the windmill. Only three blades were rotating. Three openings were possible. "Oomph, this looks tough. It is slow, but I can't underestimate it.

I just hope there is something on the other side," he said to himself. "Andrea! Does your map have anything after that giant spinning windmill?" Eric asked with concern.

"Let me check. Yeah, there's another platform across the windmill. You have to go through it."

Those were the last words Eric wanted to hear. His nerves filled him with anxiety. There was no choice but to walk closer to the dynamic structure.

As Andrea swatted off the pixies, her elbow struck one of the levers down. Tiles positioned themselves alongside Andrea. Two little black dots appeared on the map. The new layout allowed her to go to the lower level. She kept swatting at the stupid fairies that made her sneeze.

Eric looked at the daunting figure. He stepped closer and tried to see his opening. He would have to jump between the blades. Even though the windmill was moving slowly, diving through the gap seemed like threading a needle. His window of opportunity was not in his favor. He took a couple of steps back and put one foot behind the other in a stance. Eric waited for the perfect opportunity. He saw the opening approach. The moment presented itself, and Eric took that moment to run towards the blades. He jumped through headfirst with his hands clasped together. Andrea looked from above, but did not see him come out on the other side.

CHAPTER 10: A SECOND CHANCE

Andrea gasped; she couldn't believe it. Did Eric fall? Worry took over her body. The map would help her find out if he was okay. She ran over to the map and saw his red dot. It was relieving to know he was still around, but she couldn't see him anywhere. It looked like his dot was floating up, but he wasn't visible to Andrea. The unsettled feeling wouldn't go away until she saw Eric again.

She located the dot and looked at where he should have been. It looked like he was on the windmill.

"Hey, Eric, what's happening with you?"

"Um, I got stuck to the blade! It's all sticky! I almost cleared the opening, but my shoe got caught on the tip of the blade. I'm standing on the blade. It's weird. I've tried walking. It's a bit difficult. Especially missing a shoe. I have to jump on the platform when I get closer to it. I hope I can get myself off the glue."

Andrea started chuckling when she heard about his shoe. "It sounds like you're holding up well," she said. Eric didn't respond.

Andrea was struck in the face by the pixies. Andrea saw a button she hadn't seen before and it had a picture of a helmet. The button didn't give a clue, but helmets were usually associated with armor. It was worth a try.

She pressed the button, and weird sounds came from behind the panel. A tiny, cube-shaped display case popped up. It was encapsulated in a glass box. There were strips of LED lights that illuminated the inside of the box. A tiny gray cube was in the center. Andrea stared at the box. Two small robotic arms popped out from the bottom. They extended their probes and started inspecting the box. Andrea thought it was peculiar.

Andrea was hit in the face again by a fairy. Her frustration grew due to the pesky little cunts. She averted her attention from the fairies back to the box. The arms had pierced the opposite sides with their probes. Electric arcs ran along the arms, jolting into the cube. Electricity shocked the polymer structure of the cube. It activated a memory shape, and the tiny cube started to unfold. Andrea was mesmerized by the process. A physical shape transformed in front of her eyes. The structure started to stand. Mesh layers formed against the tiny tubes. A full helmet assembled in seconds. A tiny hammer extended out with a small sign underneath. *Break in case of emergencies.* Andrea read the sign and knew it was perfectly acceptable to smash the glass.

Andrea grabbed the hammer and struck the glass case. A gas dispersed, and the glass shattered into tiny pieces. She dropped the hammer and grabbed the helmet. It was grey and curvy. The visor was green and wrapped around her head elegantly. The mouth had intricate filters built into the breathing holes. She put it on without much hesitation. The helmet formed to her features; it felt organic. It wrapped around her neck, and the visor perfectly fit around her field of vision. One of the fairies flew by. It flicked its wand at Andrea's head. A puff of smoke bounced off the helmet. Andrea smiled and was excited about her new piece of equipment. A sense of immortality rushed over her. It was small, but it gave a huge boost to her psyche.

Eric waited for the platform to come by again. He counted down the seconds. The stickiness stuck like gum to his shoe. Strands trailed from his shoe to the blade. It was going to be more difficult than he had anticipated.

The ledge was getting closer. He tried to run, but the goop held him down. His legs stayed planted on the blade. Eric lost his balance and fell forward onto the sticky residue.

"Ugh, gross. What the hell is this stuff? Oh my god, it's everywhere. It's in my hair!"

Eric struggled to stand up. The idea of jumping off was not going to work anymore. The goop was like cement glue, and it would not let Eric go very easily.

The windmill was close to making a full rotation. It was almost Eric's opportunity to jump. He noticed a pole emitting light; it resembled a futuristic streetlight. Eric thought he could latch on and hopefully pull himself out of his sticky situation.

There was a second pole on the other side. If grabbing the first pole failed, he could try the second one. His moment was arising. The blade was getting close to the path. Eric's timing felt off. A little delay burrowed in his mind. Doubt started to cloud his judgement. Eric reached up for the pole. He held on for dear life. His arms became fully extended; he could feel his entire body stretching. Nitrogen bubbles popped in his spine. At first the tension felt relieving, but the pleasure turned into pain. Eric felt his stomach pulling away from his hips. His joints were at the breaking point.

Eric screamed out in agony. The sounds of bugs getting squished came from his body. Eric thought his torso was getting ripped away from his legs. His neck strained down to look at his feet. He expected to see that his legs had detached from his body while he hung onto the pole. Luckily, the sounds were coming from the strands of goop ripping. His feet were coming off the blade of the windmill.

The foot with no shoe was getting yanked by the blade. Eric had freed himself a little, butthe goop kept him from escaping. He mustered all his might. Eric pulled his foot with great strength and freed himself. His body went limp against the lamp and his legs hung off the deck. Eric pulled his legs up to the platform.

Eric lay motionless, his chest beating up and down. Catching his breath, he felt adrenaline flow through his body. His eyes stared out past a thousand yards, staring at the chance of death. A glimpse of it had been dangled in front of him. He flashed back to the dogs. Eric shuddered and shook his head out of the illusion.

Andrea stared at Eric, hoping everything was okay. One of the blades moved out of the way, and she saw a glimpse of Eric's body on the ground. The worst conclusions flooded Andrea's head with false scenarios. She would not make any assumptions until she saw him for herself. There was movement coming from his direction. The fairies kept trying to blow dust onto Andrea's face, but the mask worked flawlessly.

He rolled over onto his side. Eric could barely stand and fell to the ground. Something was wrong. Eric crawled to a wall and leaned against it. His ankle started to swell and turn purple. He looked closely at his foot. The joint was disconnected, and the ankle twisted outwards. It had popped out of the socket.

It felt like his ankle was growing to the size of a balloon. His toes lost sensation. He stared in terror until the reality set in that his ankle was completely immobile. The only thing he focused on was the angle it shouldn't have been in. He reached over with his hands and snapped his ankle back into place. Total adrenaline took over, and his body went into shock. His mind told him that his ankle shouldn't twist that way. There was no way he could continue unless he crawled.

"Andrea! My foot is fucked! I can't move it anymore. I can't put any weight on it. I will collapse. I need your help."

"Okay, stay there! Some platforms moved around on the wall next to me. I can reach you now. Let me look at the map and find a path. Hang in there, baby. I'm on my way."

Andrea shooed the fairies away while she walked towards the map. There were tiles that she could move around the map. The best plan she thought of was to get Eric onto a moveable tile. Eric was within crawling distance of a particular one. She could place him by the huge lever that had no route to it.

Andrea looked at her path. There was a gap that was wider than she could jump.

"I'm going to have to move that one closer to me. But once I jump down, I don't see how I could get to Eric's side." Andrea was stumped. "I hope there's something Eric could do on his side that will help me. It just sucks that I can't help him. He needs to go by himself. I hope he's okay with that."

Andrea went over the plan in her head before she shared it with Eric. With every passing second, the adrenaline wore off and the pain slowly crept into his foot.

"Okay, I have a plan. But you're not going to like it."

"Spill it."

"I can move one of the tiles to the end of the stretches of the platform you're on. But you need to get across the other side. I'm sorry, I can't think of anything else."

"It's okay. Where do I need to go? I can crawl well. What happens once I get on the tile? What do I do after that? I can't jump over things," Eric said.

"I can control the tile. The tile will take you across the map and under the grid. I can move you across the map to the lever."

"Oh wow, I totally forgot about the lever. Okay, that sounds like a solid plan. I have one request: move the tile in the air and wave it around so I know you're controlling it."

"Done."

The couple executed their plan. Andrea went to the light beam. She whisked her hand around the light and moved the tile. It was under her command. The tile approached Eric and started to sway back and forth. Eric crawled towards the platform. His hands grabbed the floor, and he slid his lower half across the bridge. The palms of his hands started to burn in pain.

Eric could see the tile landing. It gave him hope. If he could make it to the tile, he knew Andrea would guide him in the right direction. Andrea brought the tile level with the floor. He scooted all the way to the tile. Every inch came with rising pain. Eric finally made it.

There was a tiny gap between the tile and the edge of the platform. Eric looked down. A sinking pit was in the middle of his stomach. A shiver went down his spine and his whole body shook.

He threw the upper half of his body onto the tile and he looked at his bad leg that was motionless. The floor was too smooth to pull himself over. Eric moved his good leg towards the tile. His pantleg was a good handle with which to pull his dislocated foot over the tile.

"Okay Andrea, I'm on the tile now!"

Andrea heard Eric and levitated him across the wide opening. The platform arrived at the lever. Eric launched himself over the platform. The lever was huge, and he couldn't pull it by himself. Eric needed Andrea.

There was no other option for her. She had to move the tiles for her to jump down to Eric.

Andrea looked at the route ahead of her. There were no guard rails to prevent her from falling. If she tripped or stumbled, she could fall down the deep depths of the well. The thought didn't last very long. There were four tiles to jump down. She looked at them and it seemed manageable.

Andrea finished assessing the jump, took a step back, and tooka running start. Her right leg propelled her body and she landed with both feet on the tile. The landing wasn't smooth. The girl stumbled and regained her balance. Her left foot slid across the floor and went off the tile. Andrea yelped and quickly pulled her foot back in.

The pixies were not following Andrea anymore. She looked down and thought to herself,

Three more platforms couldn't be so bad. Andrea was ready to make the next leap. She jumped off but landed with more grace. Her feet hit first, and her knees sank in to absorb the impact. She didn't stumble forward. Andrea made her jump towards the third one. This time it was flawless. She could see Eric getting closer. He didn't look too good; she could see the pain in his body.

Andrea approached the last tile. Every fiber in her body knew she could do it. Her foot was against the edge of the tile and she jumped forward. The last tile was a skipping stone. Andrea didn't stop; she used the momentum from landing to jump forward. Andrea hopped like a bunny and made it to Eric's level.

"Andrea!" Eric cried out. "Oh my god, I finally get to see you!" She ran up to him and gave into his embrace.

"Oof, this looks like it really hurts. We have to get you help immediately."

"I will be fine for now. I already set it back into place. Whoa, where did you get that cool ·looking mask?"

"These weird fairy things came out of nowhere and started shooting me with pixie dust, and it kept making me sneeze. The machine had a button that made a mask. It helped me ward off those pixies. But let's look at this giant lever."

"It's huge."

"Look at those buttons next to it. You sit tight while I try pulling this lever," Andrea said.

Andrea walked over to the lever and tugged on it. The big switch was locked. It wouldn't budge. She thought Eric should lie down on the button.

"Oh geez, I'm sorry to do this to you, but can you go sit on the button over there? I think it will help us," Andrea asked nicely.

Eric nodded and limped to the button. When he put his weight on the button, a green vial popped out of thin air. It landed in Eric's lap. He looked at the object. It was a bright green, radioactive color. The vial looked like health from a video game.

Eric drank it and a green aura went down his throat. A mystic green swirl moved along his body until it finally found his foot. The swirl made arcs and dashes around his injured ankle. His ankle glowed green, and a bright flash went off. Eric looked back at his ankle and saw the swelling was going down. The pain was going away. The potion had healed his ankle completely. He stood up confidently.

"Wow, that was some good juice. I feel amazing now."

"Good, you deserve it." Andrea gave Eric a hug. They felt warm to each other. Eric looked at her and squeezed her hard. He showered her with kisses all over. The couple had a moment together. They knew they could finish the puzzle.

"Alright, I'll stay standing on the button. Go ahead and pull the lever."

Andrea nodded in agreement. She pulled the lever all the way down. There was a huge clunking sound.

The ground started to vibrate. The couple held onto the nearest objects. The tile started to lift off and go in another direction. The couple looked into each other's eyes and hoped for the best. The tile moved quickly through the air. The long wait came to a halt. The tile slowed down when it reached its next platform.

The couple regained their balance and walked to the end of the tile. They saw where they landed. It was next to a new platform. They walked on it and saw a big wall. In the middle of the wall was a white wooden door. Above the door was a sign. *Get out of the loop.* The couple smiled at each other. They grasped each other's hands and realized nothing could stop them.

Andrea was the first to walk through the door. She looked up in anticipation of an end, but it was just another room. Andrea sighed. Disappointment ran through her bones. One more room. This room was completely white. White floors, white walls, and a white ceiling. But it was also very bright. There was no furniture in the room. It was just one big empty room.

"I never liked the color white; it makes me feel uneasy. Nothing is that perfect and it will probably get dirty over time. It feels really eerie in here. Like an empty hospital," Eric said.

Andrea agreed with Eric. They walked around the room, but nothing stuck out. Eric stood close to a wall and put his hand on it. He pounded the wall, but it sounded solid.

"This is a weird room," Eric stated.

"So, all the other rooms seemed normal to you?" Andrea said sarcastically. Eric shot a spiteful look at Andrea. The couple walked closer together.

"We went the wrong way. They are trapping us here!" Eric yelled in agony.

"No way. There is only one door to each room. Besides, how would they benefit from kidnapping us? Our parents would start to ask questions very quickly. They won't try to kill us. No one wants to worry about a couple of dead bodies."

"They could hide our bodies," Eric said seriously. This time Andrea gave Eric a spiteful look.

A booming voice came overhead. "Hello, Andrea and Eric. You have completed The Great Escape! Congratulations, not many people make it to the end. They quit halfway into the building. Such a shame when that happens. You two are close to being done. This white room is the last room. Once completed, please exit through the giftshop. Please leave a review of your experience of The Great Escape. Thank you and have a wonderful day." The intercom announcement ended.

Eric and Andrea looked at each other and ran into each other's arms. "WE DID IT!" Eric yelled out.

"Finally! I was getting sick of all these tricks and illusions! I can't wait to eat dinner and head back home. This will be a good story to tell our friends," Andrea replied.

"Damn straight! No one is going to believe us! It's too good to be true. Frankie will probably think I was tripping balls. It was a little odd that our phones stopped working. I wanted to take a bunch of pictures and videos. I'm glad we didn't get hurt, either. Some of those rooms were dangerous. My heart was beating so fast it nearly popped out of my chest," Eric stated.

"You heard the man; this is the last room. Let's figure this thing out." Andrea turned to a door on the other side of the room. "That was definitely not in here when we first came in," Andrea commented.

Eric walked over to the door and tried to turn the knob. It did not move. "Of course it's locked! I don't know why I expected anything else."

Andrea walked over to Eric. "Don't worry, we got this," she said, and Eric nodded.

The floor started rumbling and two pillars emerged from the ground in the center of the room. The pillars were perfect white cylinders with glowing blue lights on top. The couple walked over to them. Each pillar showed the outline of a hand. The right pillar was the right hand and the left pillar was the left hand.

"I got the right side," Eric told Andrea. Andrea walked over to the left pillar. The room started to grow. The walls fled away from the couple. The white room started to transform. One of the walls turned different shades of fuchsia. The color mutated into a geometric pattern that filled in the white spaces.

It was the last knob. Chimes and bells rang down on the couple. Blue, green, and red lights shone across the ceiling. At first, they were startled and cautious. But it was true: they were done with the maze. They walked forward and saw a neon sign hung above an archway that read, *Congrats!*

Andrea and Eric looked into each other's eyes and exchanged smiles. The couple walked a little farther to find a gift shop. They were cautious of tricks planted in the room. They were scared to touch things. They started seeing the bins of themed plushies and memorabilia. There was no teller to be seen. There was only a self-service station close to the exit door.

"What do you think, Eric? They could be playing one last cruel joke on us. I really don't want to touch anything and have it send us back to the beginning of the maze."

"I get what you mean. It looks fake. Who puts a gift shop at the end of a maze? Honestly? Have you been looking at the souvenirs though? They all show something from the rooms."

Eric walked to one of the displays and saw a little shadow plushie. It had cute, bright yellow eyes and was soft to the touch.

"Oh god, not those things. They freaked the fuck out of me when they walked towards us. Huh. I don't remember them having yellow eyes though," Andrea said.

"Hm, you're right. But you've got to admit it looks pretty cute, being so small." Eric reached towards the plushie and picked it up. He looked into its eyes and pulled it towards his face. Eric pressed the plushie against his cheeks.

"So adorable! I want seventeen of them," Eric said.

Andrea looked at Eric and rolled her eyes. She wanted to see if anything had changed or was running towards them.

"I think we are safe?" Andrea said.

"I think so. Something should have happened by now. They conditioned us pretty well," Eric responded. ,

"I hate to admit it, but you're right. They totally have us all figured out. We're cautious about something that's not even there. It doesn't exist. Nothing like that can happen again. I wouldn't want my keys melting when I'm trying to get to work."

"Relax, nothing is gonna happen. They just have high tech gimmicks and tricks. I'm sure everything can be explained if we really put our minds to it."

"That's true." Andrea started to browse the inventory. She saw a rose at the corner of the store. It was a plastic rose. The petals were soft and delicate, while the stem was firm. She looked at it and rubbed her fingers against one of the petals. It was soft, but she didn't want to press any harder for fear of breaking it. The center of the rose was yellow and bright. Andrea lifted the rose to her nose and gave it a good sniff.

"Wow, this rose smells absolutely amazing. I don't think I've ever smelled anything so pleasant before." Eric walked over to see what the commotion was about. "Go on, give this a whiff!"

Eric leaned over and smelled the middle of the rose. "Wow. I wish you could smell like that. That's very therapeutic."

"Yeah, it makes you feel like you're home and safe. Nothing can hurt you any longer."

Eric saw a bin of keys. The keys were made up of different materials like jade, metal, and plastic, but they all had the same shape. He stuck his hand in and felt all the tiny pieces. All the keys were clones of each other. He picked up the jade one. Eric walked over to Andrea and asked what she was staring at.

"Look, it's a snow globe! That's cute, it has the big Connect Four bed inside."

"That is neat. I want to shake it." Eric put his hand in his pocket, then reached out to the globe and gave it a nice, polaroid-picture shake. The snow started falling onto the bed and the sides. The snow that fell on the bed glowed red and the snow that fell on the sides glowed blue. The couple was amazed.

Eric chuckled when he saw little octagons from the crazy tile room. They were coasters. "These are pretty cool! I'm actually going to get these," Eric stated.

"Well, if you're getting something, I want something, too," Andrea said.

"Well, keep looking and grab what you like," Eric mentioned.

Andrea searched the room. She wanted something small. Any of the rooms that scared her were disqualified. Andrea loved how well she worked with Eric on solving the puzzles. She felt like she could take over the world by his side. Andrea picked up a statue of the mermaid. It reminded her of their teamwork.

The couple was about to check out when a very handsome man in a well-tailored suit appeared. "Hey y'all, how'd you like the maze?" the man asked.

"It was a lot of fun. Some parts were a bit scary. But wow, I couldn't believe half of the stuff we saw in there," Eric said.

"Yes, it was beautifully coordinated. I hadn't seen anything like it before in my life," Andrea added.

"I'm so glad to hear that, folks. My grandfather has been building this attraction for years. However, it was never completed. The family hit a rough patch. I brought it back to working condition with some financing. I just wanted to say thank you for being adventurous. And my grandpa thanks you, too," Mr. Walker said.

"Your grandpa?" Eric asked.

"Yes, he was with you the whole time."

A couple wandering the streets of LA discover an enticing escape room. It is said to have law defying rooms and attractions that have never been seen before. Unknowingly, they dive into the deep wells of a maze created by a **mad man.** Each room has its own trick or game that the couple must solve to move on. Eric and Andrea use their knowledge and skills to escape a multitude of disasters that could lead to their death.

Can they survive the world's greatest escape room?

"Andrea, look at this key when I touch it. It turns into complete mush!" Her face grew puzzled. Eric was mystified by the key. "I'm going to pick it up," Eric said. He grabbed the key and set it in the middle of his palm. The bronze key turned into a bronze puddle. "It's not melting. It's cool to the touch."

$14.99
ISBN 978-0-578-89961-9
51499>

9 780578 899619